I0582606

Keep Me

A BEARS-4-U NOVEL

HJ WELCH

Keep Me
Bears-4-U

Copyright © 2023 by HJ Welch

Cover Design by Joe Satoria

This book is a work of fiction. Names, places, and incidents are either products of the author's imagination or are used fictitiously. Any resemblance to actual events, locales, or persons, living or dead, is entirely coincidental.

All rights reserved. No part of this book may be used or reproduced in any manner whatsoever without written permission, except in the case of brief quotations embodied in critical articles and reviews.

Trigger Warnings

In this book, Beckett lost his husband to cancer two years previously. He talks a fair bit about Shawn in a fond, loving way, but his grief and decision to move on is a central plot point that's featured throughout the book.

In Chapter 4, Laurie discusses some disturbing things his father said to him as a teenager. This includes how his father controlled his diet and fantasized about Laurie dying. Some readers might find the language used upsetting.

In Chapter 16, there is an on-page attempted assault and talk of a threatened sexual assault against Laurie that *does not* happen. Some readers might find the language used upsetting.

CHAPTER 1

Beckett

"HEATHER, YOU KNOW I LOVE YOU, BUT THAT WON'T STOP ME from putting duct tape over your mouth," I say dryly, not looking up from my computer and the email I need to quickly respond to.

It could actually wait. Mine isn't a life-or-death profession. I know that. But right now, I'll take any opportunity to escape my best friend's newest obsession.

My love life.

"Beck-*y*," she wheedles, dragging out the 'y' sound and using the nickname she knows I hate. "Come on. Don't get all British on me. It's been more than two years, and you know this is specifically what Shawn didn't want. For you to be slowly collapsing in on yourself like a dying star."

I wince. Sometimes Heather can be extremely American in her brutality. I try and tell myself that she doesn't have a point, but my mind trips and falters at the mention of my darling Shawn.

The man I vowed to love forever until he went somewhere I couldn't follow.

The first few months alone were the darkest. The only

thing that kept me going was how utterly furious I knew he'd be if I gave up. I promised him I'd live for us both, and now that the days are brighter, I fully intend on doing just that for as long as I possibly can.

I also promised him that I'd find love again, but I might have had my fingers crossed behind my back for that one.

How could anyone compare to Shawn? My big teddy bear. He laughed so loud and hard the whole house would shake. He adored cooking and traveling and always had something new and exciting he wanted to tell me. He was hopeless at remembering…well…anything. But that's why he had me. I kept an eye on his calendar and made sure he had enough clean socks, and helped him buy presents for his mother's birthday.

When he left me, I didn't just lose the love of my life. I lost my sense of purpose.

I scowl up at Heather, who despite my surly demeanor, is still grinning at me, holding her phone up hopefully. We're supposed to be working, but it's a slow day here at the environmental charity where we spend our days. Also, the nice thing about working for a small company is that nobody really minds a little slacking off so long as the work gets done on time.

Heather and I have been close friends for years. She was the one who got me a job here when I had to quit my old corporate life after Shawn got sick. I know she wouldn't be pushing me if she didn't think it was for my own good. And I hate to admit it, but I do desperately miss having someone dear to me that I can dote on and take care of.

As well as sex. It was the last thing on my mind for a long time, but at some point in the last few months, I do believe my libido has reawakened like a sleeping dragon, and dear *lord*, it's hungry.

"I'm fine," is what I tell her, though. Because even if I

might be getting to the point where I really need to scratch this itch, I am not going to look for someone via a *dating app.*

"Beckett, seriously," she says, raising her eyebrows, waving her phone around. "Just hear me out, okay? Yeah, you could go to a bar and try and meet some random guy, but why do that when you have such a specific type, and this bears thingy could literally find you the perfect guy in a fifty-mile radius!"

I give up and look away from the email. "I don't have a type," I say. "I had Shawn, and I'm not looking for another one of him because that man doesn't exist."

To her credit, Heather sighs and reaches out between our desks to squeeze my hand. "Of course not, sweetie," she says gently. "I would never suggest that. But Shawn had a while to think about his wishes, and he gave his explicit blessing for you to move on and find happiness again."

I chew my lip. She's not saying anything I don't know. But she's been saying it a *lot* this past week.

"Why now?" I ask curiously.

Her cheeks definitely go a bit pink. "Well, I just heard of this app," she says evasively. "I'm not sure how new it is, but it's got a lot of members already."

"And?" I say, arching an eyebrow. I can tell there's an 'and.'

"*AndImighthavesignedyouupforit,*" she mumbles, sinking slowly into her chair with each syllable as if she's hoping the fabric might absorb her.

I blink. "I'm sorry. What was that?"

She huffs and sits up again, apparently deciding to accept her fate. "I signed you up for it because I knew you never would, and well, there's this event coming up that sounded so perfect I couldn't let you miss it, but you needed a profile to apply."

"Heather," I say in exasperation. "Have you been pretending to be me and *catfishing* people?"

"No!" she cries so loudly that several other people in the open-plan office turn their heads to look or frown at us. I give them a tight smile and half a wave, and most of our colleagues get back to their own business. "No," she repeats at a more reasonable level. "Of course not. I haven't spoken with anyone. But saying that, you've still had a lot of guys wanting to match with you."

I really do scowl this time and pretend to go back to my email, even though there's no way I could concentrate on it right now. "Nope. Not interested."

"But don't you even want to know *why* this particular app is so perfect for you?" she pleads, blinking her big dark eyes at me. "Remember, I knew Shawn as well. Not to mention all the things I know about your previous boyfriends. I'm not making this up. Just hear me out."

I grit my teeth, then sigh, giving up. I know I'm a grumpy old bastard, but I remind myself that she's not trying to make me go to the dentist for a root canal. She's worried I'm lonely. That's very thoughtful of her, and there's a teeny tiny part of me that admits she sort of might be a little bit right.

"Fine," I say, stripping some of the rancor from my voice. "Why is this app different from any of the others?"

Her whole face lights up, and she kicks the floor, zooming over the few feet between us on her wheely chair, excitedly holding up her phone.

"Okay, so." She tucks a lock of black hair behind her ear. "It's called Bears-4-U. It's meant for bears and guys who are looking for bears. That's you, right? You *always* like them big, sweet, cuddly, and seriously hairy."

I can't help but snort and roll my eyes. "Fine," I concede. "Maybe I do have a type."

She holds up a finger, though, a gleam in her eye. "Ah, but this isn't just a honey pot full of beary goodness. It's kinky, too!"

I splutter. "Heather," I growl, dropping my voice down low. "I'm not *kinky*. Not really."

She arches an eyebrow at me. "Sure. Whatever you say, Daddy."

I think the blush that floods my face is humiliation I've dredged up from the depths of my very soul. I feel my mouth open and close a couple of times, but nothing comes out.

Luckily, my evil friend takes pity on me and squeezes my knee. "Relax," she says kindly. "Shawn told me once when he was extremely drunk, and I thought it was the most adorable thing I've ever heard. I haven't told another soul, I swear. And actually, that kind of thing is getting more and more common." She wiggles her phone at me. "It's kind of the point of this app."

I manage to finally take a proper breath and get some oxygen back up to my brain before I pass out. "It is?" I ask faintly.

She smiles warmly. "Yes. Look. You either sign up as a bear or a teddy bear. You're a bear—a Daddy."

"Even if I'm not actually bear shaped?" I clarify.

She nods. "I've put in your profile that you're an otter who loves bears and bear cubs. I know you hate those kinds of labels, but sometimes they're the easiest ways to communicate these kinds of things."

I grunt, choosing to gloss over that. She's right. I don't like the idea of gay men being segregated into tribes based on physical appearances. But if it means people aren't making assumptions about me, then I guess that's okay. Shawn *was* a bear and loved having that as his identity. I wouldn't want anyone to think I was appropriating that just because I'm a Daddy who likes big, hairy guys.

"And the boys are teddy bears?" I ask quietly, continuing the conversation.

I always called Shawn my teddy bear. I even laid him to

rest with his favorite stuffy to reassure myself that he wouldn't be alone in the next life. He started calling me Daddy as a kind of joke, but then it just felt right. We were never part of any community or anything, but I guess Heather's right. He was my boy.

The fact that this app should use my term of endearment for all their boys stirs something in me. Of course I meant what I said. No one could ever replace Shawn. But I can't deny that the idea of a sweet baby bear tugs at my heart-strings.

Heather squeezes my knee again. "There are all kinds of people on the app, but yes. When you fill out your profile, you can say what you're looking for. I said age didn't matter for you but that your ideal type would be a sweet teddy bear to love and spoil. I did also clearly say that you're not looking to rush into a relationship. I didn't want your inbox flooded with eager boys and for you to feel overwhelmed."

I shake my head, eyeing her phone up curiously. "I think we're probably past that point," I murmur. "But I appreciate that. Thank you."

She holds up her free hand and raises her eyebrows. "No pressure, I swear. If you want to log on, you can look at the guys who have shown you interest. Honestly, this app is so adorable. If you start a chat, they call that going into a bear cave. And looking for a match is going on a bear hunt."

She taps her toes on the carpet and does a little gleeful chair dance, and I can't help but chuckle.

"That is cute," I agree.

"But," she adds, drawing the word out and emphasizing the 't' sound, "they also have teddy bear picnics. That's where you arrange dates through the app. And it seems like the cool new thing is for venues to work with the app and set up singles mixers."

She's trying to look innocent, but now this sudden urgency all makes sense.

"Ah," I say. "Let me guess. There's an event happening near us soon?" I seem to recall she did mention something about that in her initial confession, but I blanked it out amid the horror of realizing she'd created me a profile.

She gives out a little squeal and hugs her phone to her chest. She's still only let me have a glimpse of the app in question, but at this point, I think my input isn't a requirement.

"There's a weekend mixer happening about an hour's drive out of town at this totally Instagramable lodge. Friday night to Sunday afternoon. You don't have to do *anything* or commit to *anyone*. But...I think it would be amazing if you went and just—y'know—got a feel for the vibes. If nothing else, you could go on some nice walks. Drink some wine. Perhaps even make a friend or two?"

I arch an eyebrow at her. As an extrovert, she doesn't seem to understand that I don't need a hundred friends or to be meeting new people every other week. However...the part about the nature walks doesn't sound so terrible. And it might not be the worst thing to see other men interacting as Daddies and boys. That was always something that felt very private to me and Shawn, but it's not anything to be ashamed of. Logically, I know that.

I chew on my lip for a second, then huff and hold out my hand. "Can I at least see what you've written as my profile?"

She clearly tries to contain her delight as she hands her phone over. "I used my email address and generated a random password, so I'll write that down for you now so you can log on with your own phone and change it to your email and all that. I can log off now that the cat's out of the bag, but—"

"English Dapper Daddy?" I hiss in horror when I see what

handle she's given me.

Of course she just shrugs and looks mischievous. "What? That accent is hot. You rock a vest and shirt like no one else I've ever met. You even have a god-damned pocket watch."

I glance down at my attire. I do like a waistcoat, it's true. Something about the Victorian aesthetic has always appealed to me. I'd like to think my copious tattoos offset any illusion of me being posh or fancy, though. My sleeves are rolled up to my elbows, and the full sleeves are clearly visible on my forearms.

"Fine," I grumble. She could have given me a worse username, I suppose.

I look over the bio she's written for me. It says I'm English with American citizenship looking for a sweet loving teddy bear for romance and companionship. Again, that could be worse, but I'll probably tweak it. *If* I stay on the app. Whatever.

"Where's this event?" I ask as casually as I can. My friend grins and taps on a little picnic basket icon. I realize it's already set to list by location, so the lodge in question is at the top, a different color from the rest of the links, presumably because Heather has already clicked on it.

I purse my lips and open the link up myself. Yes. It's Friday to Sunday like she said, and is being hosted in a couple of weeks. It's actually not as expensive as I thought it might have been, considering it's an all-inclusive two-night stay with a number of activities incorporated as well.

There are only three tickets left available.

I blow my cheeks out and look back at her. "I understand where the fire was."

She doesn't even look bashful as she shrugs. "There must have been a group booking or something because there have been ten tickets left for ages. But it dropped to four when I checked this morning."

I sigh. "There are only three left now."

She clasps her hands together and gives me her best Disney princess eyes. "Pleeeeease, Beckett," she whines. "Please do this for me. I won't make you do anything else ever again."

I scoff good-naturedly. We both know that's a lie. But the fact that she's so desperate for me to do this when there's nothing in it for her is extremely endearing.

I glance at the photo I keep on my desk from mine and Shawn's wedding. We both look so happy in that candid shot. She's right. He was one of the most joyful people I ever knew, and he wouldn't want me to be lonely. He'd believe I had a big enough heart to love again without ever forgetting him.

I swing around and wake up my computer, where the screensaver has kicked in—another photo of Shawn and me from our honeymoon. I'm a dinosaur, and I don't like doing fiddly things on my phone.

"You better give me that password, then, if I'm going to buy a ticket."

She keeps her mouth closed, but a little scream escapes her throat anyway. Despite everyone else in the office giving us the side-eye, she throws her arms around me and hugs me tightly. "Good man," she says sincerely. "You'll have fun, I promise."

I don't know if I'd go that far, but something within me is gently saying that it's okay. This feels right. I'm not leaving Shawn behind, but I need to stop stagnating and move on with my life as well. What better way to mark a new era than jumping in with two feet? This weekend will symbolize that.

It's not like I'm going to meet anyone, anyway. I'll just go along and get a little taste of what my life could start to look like as the new Beckett Gates.

Nice and safe. Nothing to worry about.

CHAPTER 2

Laurie

I GRIP MY HANDS TIGHTER AROUND THE STEERING WHEEL AND let out a deep breath, trying to dispel the built-up tension. "I am a good person," I say gently to myself. "I am worthy of love."

I have a few of these mantras I try and tell myself daily, but I find them hard. If I'm going to be brave, though, and really attend this event, I'm going to need all the courage I can muster. My confidence and ego are still pretty bruised, but no one is going to pull me out of this funk aside from me.

Bears-4-U has been like a breath of fresh air after the last couple of disastrous years. If there's any way I'm going to truly forget all about George, it will be by meeting someone else. There's nothing like the dizzying distraction of new relationship energy.

I glance at my phone. It's currently acting as my GPS, taking me to Shellridge Lodge, which is in the woods near Heidecke Lake, Illinois, for what could be a whole weekend of fun. I just have to hope I don't blow it by saying something stupid.

The phone is also home to my Bears-4-U app and where

I've been talking to a few different Daddies, but mostly Pancake Papa. I don't know his actual name yet, but he's the one who suggested I come to this getaway so we could meet in real life. I'm so nervous, but he really can't be any worse than George.

My throat gets tight, and I turn my music up a little to try and chase away the pain that's still horribly raw when I think about my ex. Thank god I finally saw the light and blocked his ass. But I still feel the bitter disappointment and rejection that he's left me with. A part of me always knew he was messing with me, but I thought I was in love with him, so I stuck around for almost two whole years.

Poor, stupid little me.

I rub my chest and take another few breaths. George is in the past. I'm still only twenty-five and have a big, bright future ahead of me. There are literally thousands of Daddies out there, and I'm sure they'll all be an improvement on my manipulative ex. I just have to open up my heart and let them in.

I'm trying not to get my hopes up about Pancake Papa— or just Papa, as I've been thinking of him. We've had a lot of fun chatting over the past couple of months and even sent each other naughty photos and jerked off at the same time. The thrill of clumsily replying one-handed to his messages with my other hand wrapped around my cock sends shivers down my spine now and helps chase away my melancholy.

Sure, I don't know much about Papa. He hasn't told me a lot of details about his life, which makes me nervous. But that's why it'll be good to meet in person. I can check him out face-to-face and get a feel for his vibe.

I've promised myself that if there's even a hint of a red flag, I won't talk myself around it this time. I'll walk away.

But I hope not. I've lain awake imagining that he'll be gorgeous and romantic. And the lodge where we're staying looks so pretty! I was anxious about spending all that money on just a couple of days, but my mom—bless her—bullied me into taking a day's vacation off work. She's not too up in my business, but she always says that an adorable little bear cub like me deserves a handsome boyfriend. I don't think I'm ready for a whole singles vacation—like those big cruises hundreds or thousands of guys go on around the Caribbean. But a short weekend away could be really fun.

"Fun, not stressful," I remind myself as I take the exit off Route 47 and follow the directions along some twisty, turny roads. I don't have anything to prove to anyone.

But that's my problem. I always feel like I have to be the best and try the hardest. Otherwise, it's not good enough. Like I'm letting people down. I don't know who exactly I'd be letting down at the mixer or what I'm really worried about happening. Embarrassing myself, I guess? But I have to remember that the only person I'm really here for is me.

Except...*urgh* I want a Daddy to be good for so badly. I can't help it. I crave praise and attention. That dizzying high of being told I'm good and perfect. That's all I want.

Do I deserve that, though? Am I a good person?

I shake myself in my seat and frown at the road. I'm not here to get my soul weighed. I'm here to meet Pancake Papa and maybe some other people and, y'know, perhaps get some sex. I'm trying not to get my hopes up on that front, but damn, what I wouldn't give for a Daddy to really take care of me in that kind of way.

It doesn't take much longer to get to Shellridge after the turnoff. Maybe half an hour? I kind of wish it was longer as nerves flutter like butterflies in my tummy. I rub my belly, trying to settle myself. I want to make a good first impression and not come across as the wallflower I usually am.

I park my old car in the lot, kill the engine, and take a few deep breaths. Memories of awkward school dances flood unbidden into my mind. I always went alone, of course. The chubby gay kid trying to blend into the background, always desperate to be noticed but then terrified of what would happen if I was.

At least I knew people then. I hung out with the other drama geeks and got to have a bit of a dance, even if it was never a slow one. But here...

Technically I know Pancake Papa, but not what he *looks* like. I'm hoping we'll get name tags. That seems typical for an event like this, right? But what if I go to the wrong place or miss something or...or...

Or I could just go inside. I'm here now. What are my options—sit in my car? Turn around and drive home, wasting all that money? No. As frightened as I am, I can't do that. Mama said to be myself. I'm naturally cheery when I'm not crumpling into a ball of fear. If I simply smile and be polite, it'll probably take me a long way.

Before I can change my mind, I unbuckle my seat belt, get out, and grab my small suitcase from the trunk. "I am a good person," I whisper under my breath as I lock the car, then walk over toward the front entrance. "I am worthy of love."

It's a sunny spring day. My favorite kind of weather, actually. I take a deep breath and look around at my surroundings. Shellridge Lodge is charming as hell. The main building with the reception and restaurant and such looks like the kind of log cabin you see in pictures from Switzerland or on Christmas cards. The structure is mostly wooden, with a slanted roof and a large stone chimney with smoke gently drifting out of it. I bet it's even more gorgeous when it snows, but that seems unlikely at this time of year.

The rooms are all in little chalets that look like smaller versions of the main lodge. I can just see some of them between the pine trees. The cheaper ones are clumped together in bigger blocks—that's where I'm staying. But there are other buildings that only have a couple of suites. The best ones are for individual bookings, and those are more like little houses with kitchens and fancy bath tubs and stuff. Not that I spent ages looking online, wondering if Pancake Papa might have one of the bigger rooms.

Even if I just stay in my room and go for a walk or two, this will be the closest I've gotten to a proper vacation in a long while. George kept saying he'd take me, but...

Nope. Banishing that thought. I don't need George to take me anywhere. I don't need George for anything.

"I am worthy of love," I mutter stubbornly as I stomp up the few steps toward the front door. Except I'm a little too enthusiastic with the last one, and my foot slips. My suitcase shoots backward on its wheels, taking me with it as well. I pinwheel my arms, but there's nothing to stop me from flying onto my ass.

Except...I don't. I vaguely register a shout, but it's more the strong arms that grab me that I'm paying attention to. My heart is hammering in my throat as I blink and feel myself gently tipped back onto my feet.

"You nearly took quite a tumble there," an English accent says, as smooth as silk. I gulp and am almost too afraid to turn around, but I do. The guy is only a little taller than me, with a slim but compact body. He's wearing a warm purpley-brown suit with a vest but no tie. I can see hints of tattoos peeking out from under his collar and cuffs. He's clean-shaven, but there's a hint of dark chest hair where he's left his top button undone. His smile is crooked as he steps away from me.

My knees go weak.

"S-sorry," I manage to stutter, my cheeks flaming with embarrassment. "Apparently I can fall over thin air if I really set my mind to it."

The man chuckles warmly and genuinely, not like he's

simply humoring me and my silly joke. Some of the tension in my body eases, but I bite my lip as I watch him first pick up my case, then his own.

"Thank you," I murmur, this time without stuttering. I take the handle and inhale slowly. It's okay. Nothing disastrous happened. In fact, something a little bit amazing might have just happened. Talk about a gentleman. *Wow.* He's got to be a Daddy, right?

The guy hops up the last couple of steps and holds the door open for me. I can't lie, it makes my insides melt and other parts of me go all tingly.

"There we go, safe and sound," he says.

I glance at him as I scurry inside, but I'm too shy to look for long. We find ourselves in the foyer along with a bunch of other guys, and by looking at them, I can tell they're all here for the same thing. I've never been to a bear bar or club or anything, so seeing so many guys who look like me is pretty awesome.

"Are you, um…" the British guy says, gesturing to the group.

"Uh, yeah," I say, equally awkward. "Bears-4-U?"

He chuckles. It reminds me of leaves rustling in a forest. So lovely and calming. "My friend bullied me into coming. She says this is called a teddy bear picnic."

"My mom made me come!" I say, excited that we have something in common. Then I realize in horror what I just said. How completely uncool.

But the guy's expression is fond. "That's very caring of her," he says without a trace of sarcasm or judgment. I manage a small smile.

"She'd like me to meet someone nice."

We both move forward in the line for the check-in desk. "I'm sure you've got a good chance here," he says. "Have you been speaking with anyone beforehand?"

"Uh, yeah," I say shyly. "Pancake Papa?"

I'm half hoping this is him, even though I'm sure Papa said he's got a husky build. Sure enough, this guy smiles, but there's no hint of recognition. "These handles do make me laugh. My friend picked mine. 'English Dapper Daddy.' I'll give her props for her branding being on point, I suppose." He gives me that lopsided grin again as he jabs his hand out. "You can call me Beckett, though. I imagine we'll be seeing each other around these next couple of days."

My heart aches, and I really, *really* hope that's true. But then I feel a flash of shame. I know we haven't officially committed to anything, but I'm here to connect with Papa. I shouldn't be getting my hopes up over a guy I just met, no matter how dashing he is.

"Laurie," I say as he releases my hand. I miss his warmth immediately, but we're moving forward in the line again, so it's probably for the best. "'Lil Star Bear' is my username."

He beams at me. "How charming," he murmurs. "Are you interested in astrology or star gazing?"

I wrinkle my nose. "Not really," I admit with a nervous laugh. "But I've always been, um, a bit of a daydreamer. At school, I would always rather be in the theater than in a chem lab. My teachers would always say that I had my head in the clouds, like it was a bad thing. My mom told me I had my head in the stars, and that one day I'd fly all the way to the Milky Way."

It's ridiculous, but admitting that out loud makes me a little bit emotional. I cough to try and cover it up. Mama has always believed in me, even when nobody else did. Not even myself.

"That sounds perfect," Beckett says, again without sounding like he's scoffing at me. "The world needs art just as much as science. Is that the field you work in now?"

I laugh hollowly. "Sadly, no. Right now, I work on one of

those customer service call lines. I guess it pays the bills. But I do community theater in my hometown, Alder, so that's nice."

"Certainly," Beckett says cheerfully. "Besides, you're young. You have so much time to discover what you truly want to do with yourself."

I want to ask him what he does. I want to stay talking with him all afternoon. He's made me feel so at ease in just a few short minutes. But the guy in front of us moves, and then the reception desk is free.

Beckett gestures for me to go, but then to my surprise he follows me, staying close without crowding me. The woman at the computer smiles brightly. "Hi, there," she cries. "Are you checking in together?"

"Oh, no, separately," Beckett says kindly. For a second, I wish we were checking in as a couple, but that really is daydreaming. "Why don't you go first, Laurie?" he says.

If my heart wasn't a puddle before, it is now. Not only did he remember my name, but he's now watching out for me, making sure I check in okay. How very...*Daddy* of him.

I give the lady my details, a little embarrassed that Beckett might figure out I'm in one of the cheapest rooms possible. My anxiety only gets worse when I realize *he's* in one of the best, super fancy suites. But he doesn't give any indication that it matters to him. In fact, he turns to me as we leave the desk together.

"I know you said you're meeting someone here," he says. "Did you want to rendezvous with them if they've already arrived? If not, I could perhaps escort you to your room?"

The nice check-in lady just said it could be a bit of a maze around the different buildings if you weren't careful. I appreciate his offer immensely, but then feel torn. I *should* be messaging Papa to see if he's here. But I hadn't heard anything at the point at which I left my car, and he's not in the lobby. So I figure it's not hurting anyone if I accept Beckett's kindness.

"That would be great," I say. But then I have a thought. "Oh, unless *you're* meeting anyone?"

He chuckles and starts walking toward the smaller rooms, so I follow. "Oh, no. I haven't spoken to anyone. I…well, I've had a tough couple of years. I promised my best friend that I would come and mingle, but I'm not looking to meet anyone."

"Ah," I say with a nod, really trying not to feel crushed because that's ridiculous. I just met the guy, and I actually have made plans with someone else, so there was never any reason to get my hopes up. Maybe I'm just sad in a general way. I don't like the idea of Beckett going through a bad time or being on his own.

"So the Pineapple Papa guy," Beckett says, making me burst out laughing. "What?" he asks.

"Pancake," I tell him between giggles. "Pancake Papa."

He once told me that's his name because he likes to flatten good boys like pancakes. That made me feel a bit funny. I know things get lost in translation online, so it was probably meant to be sexy. But it did kind of sound aggressive. I'm more than likely just being overly cautious for obvious reasons. I focus now on Beckett.

He grins bashfully. "My mistake. This guy. Are you involved? Have you met before?"

There goes my heart again. He's worried about me meeting a stranger from the internet, I'm sure. "No, we haven't met," I admit. "But that's kind of why we've come here. It feels safer. In fact, I think that's the point of having picnics via the app in the first place. It means there's some accountability."

"Absolutely," Beckett agrees. We stop outside my building

and pause a little awkwardly. "Well...this is you, isn't it?" I nod. "Are you coming to the welcome buffet later?"

"Yes," I say brightly, hoping I'll be able to see him again. Unless I get whisked off my feet by Papa, I suppose. "That's where we get our lanyards and those bingo cards to encourage us to talk to people, right?"

"I believe so," he says. There's another pause, like he doesn't want to leave. But then he gives a little shake and beams at me. "I'll let you freshen up. It was a pleasure to meet you, Laurie, and if I don't catch you later, good luck meeting your Daddy."

I smile, but I can tell it doesn't meet my eyes. Pancake Papa is definitely not my Daddy. Not yet, anyway. Maybe I'll get lucky. Who knows? But as Beckett gives me a small wave and wanders away, I can't help but feel he's taking a little bit of my heart with him.

Absurd. We just met, and I'm interested in someone else. He was just being genuinely nice, and after George, that seems like an alien concept. Besides, Beckett made it clear that he's not looking for anyone this weekend.

I let myself into the front door of the communal chalet and try and brush it off. A quick shower and a change of clothes are what I need. Then I'll be ready to meet my maybe-Papa and really get this weekend started.

Whether or not it has any more of the English Dapper Daddy in it.

CHAPTER 3
Beckett

OH.

Oh, no.

I realize I've been sitting on the end of my bed for good-ness knows how long, twisting my wedding ring on my finger. Heather gently suggested taking it off before I came, but the idea made me feel physically sick, so she very quickly backed off. I swallow now and look at the platinum band that's meant so much to me for so long.

And then I think about Laurie.

It's almost as if that makes my heart actually ache in my chest, and I take a second to rub my sternum. I came here planning to observe. To maybe talk to some other Daddies and get a feel for the community.

Not to rescue the first boy I laid eyes on and let him totally capture my heart.

No, that's ridiculous. I'm just so long out of the dating game that I'm getting confused. Besides, I have natural caretaking instincts. That's probably what it is. That young man screamed to be taken care of, and I got to do it for fifteen minutes. It's been two years since I had that pleasure, and my brain is just probably flooded with dopamine right now.

Then why can't I get those green eyes or that shy smile out of my head? That story about being a daydreamer tugged at my heart strings. Shawn was a kindergarten teacher, and he never stopped being a big kid. It scares me how I've let that joy fade from my life. He was the chaos and color to my order and reliability. That's why we worked.

I like that Laurie is drawn to the theater.

And another man.

He's already meeting someone, so I need to stop this nonsense right the hell now. I slap my knees and make myself stand, stretching my stiff arms out and making my neck crack. I wander over to the window and look out at the sloping forest and picturesque landscape. The lake is just visible in the distance. The sky is blue for now. However, there's supposed to be a storm coming in over the weekend. I trust my Jeep to handle most things, but even after so many years in this country, I still sometimes find myself caught out by the extreme weather.

I have to laugh. You can take the man out of Great Britain but not the Brit out of the man. I don't want to think about an uncomfortable situation, so my mind latches on to talking about the weather, even if it's only to myself. How dreary.

Laurie didn't make me feel dreary, though. In fact, quite the opposite. That's probably the most alive I've felt since we got Shawn's diagnosis. I glance up at the ceiling, my throat feeling tight. "What do you think, darling?" I ask.

I don't expect an answer of any kind. I'm not particularly religious. I don't really know what I believe happens to our souls when we leave this earth. But I do still talk to my husband quite a lot, hoping he's checking in on me from time to time.

I wish he could talk to me now, though, just for a

moment. I'd love it if he could reassure me that what I'm doing is okay. But Heather was right. He was incredibly clear that he didn't want me to be the kind of widower that gets stuck and can't move on. He always had so much love in his heart. I'm sure he'd be all right with me loving again. In fact, before our lives got turned upside down, he'd mentioned many times that if we ever found a third, he would be more than willing to consider opening up our marriage.

I twist my wedding band again, feeling like he's here with me in some way. Goodness, I knew this was going to be a challenge, but I didn't expect to be blindsided at the very first hurdle. Perhaps it'll get easier from here on out.

I guess first things first, I should get ready for this mingling thing they're going to force us to do. I know the entire point is to meet people, but the idea of making point- less small talk with strangers sounds completely draining. I suppose that's what I was doing with Laurie just now, but that didn't feel like a chore at all.

I almost wish it was just him I was going down to meet, but I catch myself before I do. He's off limits until he meets this Pancake man.

Oh.

It's bad, but the idea that I can go and keep a casual eye on him spurs me to start pulling my clothes off. Yeah. I'll just make sure everything's okay with him, then I can try and talk to some other people.

I've done most of a day at work as well as the drive from the city out to the sticks, so a freshen-up would definitely be a good idea. I wouldn't mind a slightly more casual outfit, either. It's bad enough that I feel like a bore. I don't want to look like one as well.

I'm jittery, so I don't hold back from a quick shower wank. I try to keep my mind clear, just imagining a hot mouth instead of my palm as the water cascades down my body. But I can't deny the image of fluttering blond eyelashes that creeps in just as I come all over the tiled wall. I breathe heavily and blink as my seed gets washed away. Well…that was almost something to feel guilty about. Best not to examine it too closely.

Instead, I find a pair of navy trousers, pair them with a light blue shirt and darker waistcoat, make sure my shoes are shined, then spritz on some cologne. As I'm not adding a jacket, I roll up the shirtsleeves and fasten on one of the watches I brought with me. I decided against bringing the pocket watch, as if people don't know me it can make me seem like a bit of a pretentious twat. I do have a couple of expensive ones with me, but this is my favorite, as Shawn got it for me. There we go. Another way to feel like he's here with me in spirit.

I wonder what he might think of Laurie. Would they get along? I try and remind myself that I need to keep my distance and let the young man meet his online friend, but that's overshadowed by the idea that together, despite their age difference, the two boys would have shone like the sun.

"Enough," I grumble. I grab my wallet, phone, and room key, then stomp out the chalet door before I can think up any more nonsense.

The temperature has dropped as evening's come in, but it's still gorgeous and fresh. If nothing else on this weekend away, a shake-up of scenery has got to do me some good. I inhale deeply, filling my lungs with cool air and a sense of hope that I haven't felt in a long time.

Change is coming, one way or another. And I think I'm finally ready for it.

Back in the main lodge, there's a small room that's been set up for people to register and pick up their name tags, as well as the bingo card that we're supposed to fill out by finding people who can tick off all the boxes. The table is being manned by a couple who I'm almost certain are Daddy and boy by the way the cheeky, excitable cub keeps getting told off by the older bear. I could be wrong, but I think they're both enjoying the telling-off a *lot*.

I slip the lanyard over my head, noting that it says both my name and user handle. I cringe slightly, but I guess it isn't the worst. Heather could have fucked me over a lot more, and I appreciate that she didn't. She genuinely wants this to work for me.

I sigh. I sincerely doubt I'm going to be able to return home and tell her I made any real connections, but the fact that I'm here is a huge step, and we both know it. I decide to try my best to fill out the bingo thing, but first, I definitely need a drink.

The mixer event is focused in the lounge area where the bar is located. They've also set a buffet up for us, and there are a lot of people already congregating around small tables in a mismatch of comfy-looking armchairs and sofas. I scan the room but don't see Laurie. I remind myself that's fine— he might well have met up with his internet Papa already. I need to be more concerned with myself.

That starts with a nice glass of something strong and red. I already looked at the wine list when I made the booking and was pleased to see that someone here obviously knows what they're doing. I select a Chilean merlot and savor the first sip before moving around the room in the general direction of the food. But as I pass one of the many large potted plants, a familiar voice arrests me from the other side.

"I am a good person," Laurie whispers earnestly. "I am worthy of love."

I freeze, hidden by copious leaves, then sink into the mercifully empty armchair next to the pot. I can barely see him, and I'm certain he hasn't noticed me, but I'm ninety-nine percent confident that it's him, even though we only spoke for maybe fifteen minutes at most. Those words just now, though, have pierced my heart, and it's like I'm powerless to leave. I can just about see that the seat beside him at the small coffee table is empty, so perhaps he's meeting his maybe-Daddy for the first time.

It's a private moment. I shouldn't intrude. And I won't. But right now, I can't leave him, not when he's all alone. So I place my wine glass down and lace my fingers together, taking a couple of deep breaths. I'll just watch over him until his date arrives, then I'll know he's okay. That's all.

I promise.

CHAPTER 4

Laurie

I FIDDLE WITH THE CARROT STICK I'M CURRENTLY SWIRLING IN Thousand Island dip. I should be hungry. I haven't eaten since breakfast. But I'm so nervous and confused that I've ended up with a plateful of yummy-looking food, and yet I've barely touched it.

I'm meeting Pancake Papa any minute now, but I can't stop thinking about Beckett. I'm trying to tell myself that's because I have a face to put to Beckett's name. I know the sound of his voice. Despite us corresponding for months, Papa feels a lot less real to me in this moment compared to Beckett.

Hopefully that will change. I don't want to mess him around over a guy I met for all of fifteen minutes. I told him where I'll be and what I'm wearing. It's silly, but even though we're about to meet, I didn't feel like I could send a photo, and he didn't offer one up either. I'm wondering if that means something or if I'm just reading too much into every tiny little detail.

I'm certainly distracted. I don't even notice the man who approaches me until he speaks.

"Star Bear?" a deep voice rumbles.

My head snaps up, and I see a proper bear of a man looming over me. He's broad and solid with a full, dark beard and a lumberjack shirt buttoned up over his round belly. The baseball cap he's wearing partially covers his face, but that's okay. Excitement bubbles in me anyway.

"Pancake Papa?" I ask, jumping to my feet. Then I blush, unsure of what to do next. Hug? Shake hands? High-five? In the end, he solves the dilemma for me as he grunts and takes the seat I've been saving for him. "Hi," I add weakly before also sitting back down.

"Hey, cutie," he says with a big smile, and some of the tension leaves my body. I can see a bit more of his face now as he pushes his cap back. "Nice to finally meet you. You sure are something. You find the place okay?"

I breathe out. Right. He seems nice. Maybe a little abrupt, but I like that he asked about my drive. "Yeah, I just followed the GPS for an hour or so, no problem. You?"

He shrugs. "Kind of a bitch. I left home at the ass crack of dawn. But this was close to you, so it seemed like a good idea at the time. Hey—you want a beer?"

I swallow and nibble my lip. I wasn't sure I wanted to drink tonight. I'm so nervous, and I want to make good decisions. But I don't want to turn him down or make him feel bad either. "Uh...maybe in a minute. I'm Laurie, by the way."

"Oh, right! Yeah!" he cries, shoving his hand toward me. "Michael—or Mick, if you like. I guess you can just stick with Papa, though, right?"

He winks, but something in me shivers just a little—in a cold way, not a delicious way. It might not be a full-on red flag, but assuming that I'll just want to call him Papa or Daddy feels a bit weird.

"So, beer?" he says with raised eyebrows.

"That's so nice, thank you," I say, remembering my

manners. "But would you mind if I just started with a lemonade?"

He shrugs again. "If you want. I see you already attacked the buffet." He leans over and peers at my plate. "Although I don't know what you're doing with all those veggies and salad and shit." He grins at me, but there's something feral in it that makes me shrink back slightly. "How about we get rid of that, and I pick up a nice stack of cakes and cookies? Gotta keep you sweet and plump, right?"

Before he's even finished speaking, blood is rushing through my ears, and I'm feeling faint. I grip onto the table, acid churning in my stomach as I look down at all the food I selected for myself. The thought of eating anything right now is impossible, though. My mouth is dry, and I'm taking shallow little breaths.

"N-no thank you," I manage to stammer.

He scoffs. "Aren't you supposed to do what Papa says? I thought you were a good boy? Am I going to have to punish you? That fat ass looks like it could use a spanking."

Tears are burning in my eyes. What the hell? I never said anything about wanting spankings or being fat-shamed or any of this! I *definitely* don't want him telling me what I can and can't eat. Humiliation is flushing through me, and I try not to panic. I want to be a good boy so badly, but what he's asking of me is too much.

"S-sorry," I say, still stuttering. "I don't want...I mean...I can't..."

He scowls at me. "Spit it out, boy. Tell you what. You stay here, and I'll take care of the drinks and food as that's what Papas do. Then we can maybe continue this conversation in my room." He gives me that scary grin again. "Unless you'd like me to punish you in front of all these good folks?"

I think I'm going to pass out. I'm actually *frightened*. I don't like what he's doing, but I'm not sure how to make him stop without being rude. I am absolutely not going to his room, though. That's for sure.

"I-I…no…I…"

His expression suddenly changes, and he frowns as he looks up over my shoulder. "Can I help you?"

"Yes, I rather think you can," an English voice says cheerfully, and my heart almost stops.

Oh no!

Mick raises his eyebrows and throws out his hands. "And?"

"And you can *fuck* off," Beckett says in that same cheerful tone. I'm so stunned by the curse that I snap my head around to look up at him, causing the tears that were precariously teetering on my lashes to tumble down my face. He's got his hands in his pants pockets, and he rocks easily on the balls of his feet, but his smile doesn't reach his blazing eyes.

Mick splutters. "We're having a private conversation, jackass. How about *you* fuck off all the way across the pond?"

"Not that private, I'm afraid," Beckett says, like he is actually sorry. "I heard every word. Let me ask you—what part of 'no' was unclear?"

Holy shit. If I thought I was embarrassed before, that's nothing to the mortification that rinses through me now. He heard all of that? I can't think of anything worse.

"Listen, buddy," Mick says threateningly, rising to his feet. I shrink back against my seat, but Beckett doesn't flinch a muscle.

"Oh, I'm listening," he says pleasantly. "I listened to the part where this charming young man refused you *three* times, and yet you insisted on pushing on. Let me ask—is humiliation part of his kink requests? Because looking at his face, I'd guess not. And that would mean you were trying to force him into something he didn't consent to. I wonder what the event organizers would think about you breaking their most fundamental rule?"

Some of the bluster seems to evaporate from Mick as he stares at Beckett in horror. "That's not what's going on here. We know each other!"

"Well, so do we," Beckett says, finally sounding furious. "And that is *no* way to treat a boy who clearly isn't interested in what you're offering. You're supposed to take care of him, not trigger a panic attack."

"A what?" Mick scoffs. "He's not some little pussy. He's fine!"

"Clearly," Beckett says dryly. He looks down at me at last, and I suddenly feel like I can breathe again. "Sweet boy, it's up to you. If you're okay here, you can of course stay. Or you can come with me right now somewhere quiet and calm where we can talk this all through."

I'm so ashamed, but a sob escapes my throat. "Yes, that," I manage to stay. "Yes, please. Thank you, Beckett."

He holds his hand out to me, and I seize it gratefully as I get to my feet.

"What the fuck?" Mick explodes, making several people who weren't already looking our way snap their heads toward us and frown. "He's here with me! You can't just take him!"

Beckett hugs me tightly to his side. "I'm not taking him. I asked him, and he made a choice. I suggest that before you engage with anyone else here this weekend, you brush up on what the hell it means to be given the utmost responsibility of being anyone's Dom. Because right now, you are a walking trauma waiting to happen."

Mick looks incredulously between me and Beckett before sneering. "Fine. You want him? Take him. Little cock tease."

Beckett doesn't respond at all. He just turns us around and steers us away. It's a good thing he's clinging so tightly to me. Otherwise, I don't think my legs would be supporting me, they're so weak.

"I'm sorry," I manage to utter.

He marches us through the open doors of the dining room toward the much quieter lobby. "Sweet boy, you haven't got the slightest thing to be sorry for," he says firmly, giving my side another squeeze as he leads us into a secluded little corner behind another tall and leafy potted plant. There's an open fireplace next to us glowing with warm embers, and suddenly I feel like I've slipped into a hot bath.

I practically dissolve down onto the sofa with him. He releases my side but quickly takes both my hands in his, looking me deep in the eyes with beautiful hazel irises.

"How are you feeling, Laurie?" he asks. I kind of want to keep being 'sweet boy,' but I guess he's being really serious after that bullshit Mick just pulled, so I appreciate that a lot.

"Shaken," I say honestly, my voice sounding tight. Another couple of tears fall down my face, but I don't want to let his hands go, so I leave them to drip from my chin.

My heart almost stops when he immediately lets one of my hands go to gently wipe the tears from under my jaw with the knuckle of his index finger. No one's ever done anything like that for me before. It's so intimate for such a simple act.

He looks pained as he retakes my hand and purses his lips for a second. "Now I *am* sorry. I should have interjected sooner. But I didn't want to spoil anything if you were enjoying the back-and-forth."

I swallow, shame swooping through me again. "No," I admit with a shake of my head. "I didn't like it. He was kind of bossy over the app, but it was more sexy than aggressive, I guess. That was...horrible." I whisper the last word, afraid I might start crying properly if I think too much about it. "But don't you be sorry," I add, suddenly worried. "You saved me. Thank you. I didn't know how to escape that."

He clenches his jaw and blinks. "You shouldn't have had to go through it at all," he says, his voice hoarse. I'm glad he doesn't try and take the blame again. He really was amazing just now—all the time, actually. "I would very much like to give you a hug, if that's all right with you?"

I'd been feeling so tight in my chest, but he goes and melts my heart again like butter. "I'd love that," I tell him.

He slips his arms around me and pulls me against his solid chest. I tuck my head against his neck, and he starts carding his fingers through the short hairs on the back of my neck. I shiver—this time in the *best* way—and relax further against him.

We stay like that for a while before he speaks. "Laurie?"

"Hmm?"

"I think you might be in a form of mild shock. I'd really like to get you something sugary to eat or drink. But I meant it when I said I heard everything back there, and I would hate to upset you or overstep by selecting the wrong thing. I'm just worried."

A few more tears escape my eyes as I scrunch them together, feeling completely overwhelmed for a moment or two. The abhorrence I'd felt with Mick is still fresh, but I'm also taken aback by just how thoughtful Beckett is.

He's what a Daddy *should* be like.

I pull back and take a big, shaky breath, feeling a little more clearheaded. I wipe my face and smile at him. "Thank you. I'm a bit complicated."

He briefly cups my cheek before squeezing my shoulder. "All the best people are. Why don't I tell you what I'd like to get you?" I nod. "I think you need a hot chocolate. The heat will warm your insides, and the sugar with help your blood levels after that fright. But I know you didn't just want sweet treats for dinner, so perhaps I could get you some sandwiches as well?"

I bite my lip and breathe through my nose for a few moments. "I could have the hot chocolate first," I say slowly. "Then maybe some savory food and a soda?"

He beams at me. "Wonderful," he says enthusiastically. "I saw carrot sticks on your plate. Would you like more of them?"

I nod shyly. He seems so excited to try his best to get me what I need. "Yes, thank you. And some of that pink dip, maybe?"

"Of course. Whatever you want." He gets his phone out. "I would also like to swap numbers. If anyone approaches you while I leave you alone, you can call me. Okay?"

I feel so much safer now, but I appreciate the reasoning behind his suggestion. So we each read out our digits, and he gets me to call him for a second so we know it's worked.

"Excellent. I'll be right back."

I watch him jump up and march back toward the dining room, then turn my head to look into the low flames flickering in the fireplace.

God, I'm exhausted.

Looking back on it, Pancake Papa probably did have some red flags that I still managed to ignore, despite promising myself I wouldn't this time around. He was always pushy, and things had to be done his way all the time and on his schedule. I told myself that Daddies were just authoritative in that way.

Beckett isn't like that.

I'm not sure how long I spend with my gaze lost on the fire, but I stir as I sense movement near me. Thankfully, it's Beckett, and he's got a tray loaded with stuff that he carefully places down on the coffee table in front of the sofa.

My eyes go wide.

He not only got me hot chocolate but there's also a little side cup of whipped cream covered with rainbow sprinkles. He must have remembered that I asked Mick for a lemonade because he's got me one of those as well. My plate of food has so many of the items I originally picked, and nothing on it I don't like. He also has his own plate of food and a glass of red wine.

"I wasn't sure if you wanted cream or not," he says as he sits himself back down and holds up a spoon like a conductor's baton. "But we can add it if you want."

I feel all warm and gooey and wonder how such a similar interaction can go so right when not ten minutes ago, it just went so horribly wrong.

"I'd love that, thank you," I say coyly.

He grins and reaches for the little cup, scooping out all of the thick cream and multicolored little candies, carefully depositing the lot on top of my drink. Then he hands it over to me. He watches me take a sip, then when he's apparently satisfied, he leans back against the sofa.

"How are you doing now, sweet boy? Do you want to have dinner together, or would you like to be left alone?"

"No, don't go!" I cry, almost slopping hot chocolate all over myself.

He jerks forward and steadies my arm before giving me a warm smile once both I and my drink are safe. "I'm right here. It's fine. This is exactly where I want to be. I just needed to check I wasn't crowding you."

I nod and look sheepishly into my drink. "I'm sorry for being so much trouble," I mumble.

But when I finally look up at him again, he shakes his head. "Not at all. I'm very glad to be here with you. I won't lie —I didn't like that Pineapple chap at all."

He winks at me to let me know he got the name wrong on purpose, and I giggle, feeling slightly more at ease.

Okay. I have to trust that I'm not being a burden. I sip my cocoa and look at him. He seems to be in no hurry to eat or drink. He's just watching me like a...well, like a Daddy.

"Do you want me to explain?" I ask tentatively.

He reaches over and squeezes my leg, rubbing his thumb against my knee. I'm just wearing a pair of jeans and a white shirt. Some of the other boys are running around in cute, shiny, tiny things. But sitting here with Beckett in his pants and button-down, I feel like I chose my outfit perfectly. I like feeling his touch through the denim.

"I absolutely want to talk about it if that's what you want, Laurie," he says. "But you don't owe me an explanation."

I nod, deciding I want him to know so he can understand me better. I launch into the story, looking at my cocoa and the melting cream so I don't chicken out when I see the pity on his face.

"I'm sure it's not a surprise, but I was a chubby kid. When I hit puberty, my dad tried to force me to play football. He used to tell me all the time that he wanted a star athlete." I try not to grimace too much at the bitter memory. "I hated it. But what was way worse than being made to run laps was when he started trying to control what I was eating."

I pause, taking a second to swallow and collect myself. Beckett doesn't interrupt. He just keeps up that rhythmic rubbing of his thumb against my knee.

"At first, Mom went along with it. She's quite big as well and she tried to make it sound like we'd all be better off for it. It's not like my dad was even skinny. But he got obsessed. He weighed me every day and screamed all the time about how I wasn't losing any weight, even though I was hungry *all* the time."

I sniff, feeling so sorry for little boy Laurie. I was so achingly miserable during that time.

"What happened?" Beckett prompts.

I let out a shaky breath. "I collapsed at school. Mom was terrified that they'd call social services, and told my dad it all had to stop. She knew I didn't want to play football. I wanted to be in the drama club. She was so brave. That's the only time I remember her standing up to him about anything."

I don't try and stop the couple of tears that fall at that point. I just brush them away with my free hand, determined to get through the next part of the story as fast as possible.

"He lost his temper really badly. I think a lot of his frustrations about being 'trapped with a wife and kid' all came out. He said he fantasized about us being killed in a car crash so that he could be free."

"Oh, Laurie," Beckett says softly, and I glance up to see his eyes wide with horror.

I shake my head. It's a long time ago now, and I just want to put it behind me.

"I thought my dad was mad, but then Mom *lost* it. She started screaming at him to get out until he did. Then she got her brother to come change the locks even though it was the middle of the night. Over the next week, she boxed up all my dad's stuff and found a lawyer. They were divorced by the end of the year."

"Did you feel like that was your fault?" Beckett asks gently, and I have to laugh, even if it is hollowly.

"Fuck no," I say. "He brought it on himself, and without him, Mom and I were ten times happier. We went back to eating normally. And I know people look at us and assume it must be all junk food, but she's a great cook, and I like fruit and veggies and salad, I swear."

At that, Beckett frowns. "You shouldn't have to justify your eating habits to anyone," he says firmly.

I shrug. "I know. But I don't want anyone judging my mom. She loves me more than anything."

"That much is extremely obvious," Beckett says warmly.

"And if I might be so bold as to say that I think you are gorgeous exactly as you are."

I blush from head to toe, I'm sure. I'm still not used to compliments, but I do actually quite like the way I look. It was hard during school, but realizing that I was a bear cub—that I belonged to a specific group of gay men—boosted my confidence immensely. Especially when Bears-4-U came out, and I saw just how many guys genuinely desired people like me.

"Thank you," I manage to mumble with a smile, and he beams back at me.

But then something completely pulls me out of the lovely moment we're having.

I notice the wedding ring on his hand.

CHAPTER 5
Beckett

I realize the precise moment that Laurie's eyes go wide, and follow the direction of his gaze.

"Ah," I say, slowly withdrawing my hand.

"Are you married?" he asks bluntly with not too small a hint of accusation in his tone, and I wince. This is exactly what Heather was worried about, but I'd foolishly thought I could explain before any harm was done.

The anger in Laurie's eyes hurts me in so many ways.

"I…yes," I say, unable to say I'm not. "I was," I amend, even though I despise the use of the past tense. But this young man was so courageous, sharing his story. I need to be honest with him as well. "Can I explain?"

He clenches his jaw, clinging tightly to his mug of hot chocolate. "Okay," he says stiffly.

I don't blame him for being upset in the slightest. In fact, I'm furious at myself for causing him even more anguish on a night that has already tried him too far.

"His name is…was…Shawn. My beautiful teddy bear."

I feel my throat tighten and my eyes get wet, but I don't fight it. I want Laurie to see this side of me, the grief that I usually hide so meticulously away.

"Was?" he repeats, his voice immediately softer. Bless him. He really is very sweet and thoughtful.

I nod. Once, this conversation would have completely destroyed me. But I twist the band now, looking down at it, and feel a little surge of comfort from what I imagine to be Shawn's presence. It gives me the strength to continue.

"He passed about two years ago after a battle with cancer. I loved him very dearly. He was my whole world."

This time it's Laurie who reaches out and squeezes my knee in comfort. "I'm so, so sorry," he says sincerely. "That must have been so hard."

I sigh heavily and nod again, but I'm still smiling a little. Shawn would be proud that I'm holding my shit together. "I can't describe the agony. But every day, inch by inch, it aches a little less, and things seem the tiniest bit brighter. Until one day, I found myself here, afraid but determined."

"That's why you weren't sure about coming to the retreat," Laurie says slowly as he nods. "And why you're not in a rush to meet anyone."

I chuckle and manage a small smile for him. "Yeah. But my best friend was right. I have to start living my life again, one baby step at a time."

He rubs his thumb against my knee like I did for him. "I hope it's not patronizing to say that I'm proud of you," he says tentatively.

I place my hand over his. He automatically turns it so we're palm to palm and our fingers interlace. "Not at all," I say genuinely. "Thank you."

He takes a deep breath then puts his drink down before looking me straight in the eyes. "I probably overreacted… because my last Daddy was married. To a woman. He was having a secret affair with me."

I can tell this is a huge deal for him, so I rub my thumb

against his knuckles and give him a little nod. "Okay," I say without judgment.

It's clear he's judging himself enough. He looks stricken. "I know it was a terrible thing to do. I had no idea when we first met. But then I saw a photo of his daughter on his phone, and it all came out."

He grits his teeth and looks into the fire as he shakes his head. "I'm listening," I assure him. "Go on, please. It's all right."

"It's not all right, though. I found out he had a kid, and I didn't even put the brakes on. I thought he loved me. I'd never had a Daddy before, and some of it was absolutely magical. He took care of me and spoiled me and made me feel so important. He also *swore* he was going to leave his wife, and I kept believing him. He told me he just had to wait for the right time because of his daughter."

"Oh, sweetheart," I say, already completely unsurprised by where this tale is heading.

He rolls his eyes and gives a sad laugh. "Yeah. I was an idiot. Of course it was always the next excuse then the next… finally I cracked and confessed everything to my mom. She helped me see sense, and I broke up with him. I went totally cold turkey, which was awful, but…well, having just heard what you've been through, it doesn't seem so bad now. Besides, I probably deserved it for what I did to that poor, unsuspecting woman."

Anger flashes through me, and I reach up and touch his chin to make him look at me. "No. Absolutely not. You didn't cheat. He did. You didn't lie. He did. You believed him when he tricked and manipulated you, and that just makes you a trusting person. You were young and innocent, and he took advantage of you. I'm just glad you got yourself out of that situation."

"Thank you," he says after a few moments of consideration. Then he laughs, breaking the tension that's descended over us. I'm glad. "Oh, dear. What a pair we are."

That makes me laugh as well, then I hum in agreement. "I don't know what you're talking about," I say glibly. "I bet no one's having a sexier conversation than us."

He drops his head back and laughs, then looks back down to smile kindly at me. "It's okay, Beckett. I've heard what you've said. You're not ready for anything new, and quite frankly, I'm still a bit of a mess. We probably both need to take baby steps right now."

I sigh and think about what he's saying. Obviously, he's right. But that doesn't mean I want to chase him off.

"Perhaps baby steps could involve going for a walk tomorrow?" I suggest, hoping I'm not giving him mixed messages.

"Just the two of us?" he says hopefully, and I have to smile.

"Yes, if that's okay?" I ask. "But there are some activities during the day as well. Some sexy things like bondage displays, and also some more innocent, like life drawing or charades."

He snorts naughtily, and I can't deny something stirs within me. "I think both of those activities are probably going to get sexy as well, Beckett," he says, practically glowing with mischief.

My heart aches. I'm so incredibly grateful that I was in the right place at the right time to stop that brute from seriously hurting this sweet little cub too badly. I'm quite tempted to report Michael anyway, if I'm honest, because the thought of unleashing him on another boy is mildly terrifying. I guess there are some subs who would enjoy being treated that way. But the fact that man couldn't see that Laurie wasn't one of them doesn't fill me with confidence.

"Well," I say, "either way, I'd like to spend a little more time together as friends, if that's all right with you?"

To my relief, he nods warmly. "I'd like that as well."

I glance over at what I collected from the buffet. "Shall we start by having dinner? We could stay here or head back into the dining hall. I think the bingo card game is in full swing, and it looked like they were setting up for a quiz or a raffle or something."

He picks up his hot chocolate again and takes a gulp. My heart contracts as he accidentally gets a little cream on the tip of his nose. "Out here is fine," he says with a shy smile.

I hum in agreement before leaning forward. I love that he trusts me and doesn't move as I carefully wipe the cream off with my thumb. He giggles when I show it to him.

"I'm happy out here as well," I admit.

I wasn't particularly interested in making a bunch of new friends like I'm sure Heather would be doing in there right now. I was fine by myself. But now I've met Laurie, I want to savor every moment I have with him.

I'm worried we're treading a precarious path, but selfishly I can't bring myself to walk away from the only person to ignite any kind of fire in me for the first time in so long. The fact that he's also aware he needs to heal and wants to be cautious encourages me, especially after that close call he had with that man Michael just now.

Maybe together we can tentatively explore a friendship and enjoy this retreat as a little broken pair. And just *maybe* by the time we leave, we'll be slightly less broken, like those Japanese vases that have their cracks filled in with gold. The pain will certainly never leave me. But perhaps I might be lucky enough to discover some joy in my life again.

I have a feeling that if anyone can coax it out of me, it will be Laurie. We'll just have to see how the next couple of days go.

CHAPTER 6

Laurie

"THIS IS NOT A DATE," I MUTTER TO MYSELF AS I LEAN DOWN and tie my laces. "This is *not* a date."

Logically, I know this. I love that Beckett was so clear in communicating to me where he's at. After George, I'm very scared about being lied to or messed with. But Beckett isn't like that. I'm so glad he told me all about Shawn and his heartbreak when he died. I can't imagine losing someone I love in that way. Beckett is a very strong person.

And I was right in what I said about being kind of a mess myself. My ex clearly did a number on me. The moment I saw Beckett's wedding ring almost gave me a heart attack. Not to mention the disaster I almost walked into with Mick. I'm obviously still not recovered enough to be making big decisions.

But none of that matters when I think about Beckett's lopsided grin or smooth English voice. Or the way he held me yesterday evening like I was precious. Or how he insisted on looking after me with such care as if it was the greatest privilege in the world.

He's such easy company. We sat there for hours in that

cozy corner of the lobby by the fireplace. Once we'd finished dinner, he got up again to fetch us both fresh drinks and a plate of little desserts to share. I know my relationship with food is complicated, but so far, he's navigated everything in a way that makes me feel nurtured and understood instead of a burden.

He's addictive.

And I know I can't have him.

Which is *fine.* I completely respect the boundary he's put in place. Two years seems like a long time to me, but on the other hand, I'm not sure anyone ever completely heals from a loss like that. I would absolutely hate to make him feel uncomfortable or pressured.

But I'd be an idiot if I tried to convince myself that I wasn't incredibly, insatiably attracted to him.

I pause before tying up my second sneaker and take a moment to just sit and think about those tattooed arms of his. He seems so elegant and gentlemanly, but then he's covered in ink, and the contradiction does something powerful to my insides.

He said all the best people are complicated. I think I might have to agree.

I glance at the clock on the bedside table and yelp. I'm going to be late if I don't get a move on. I finish tying my laces, grab my jacket, and check my hair in the mirror, smoothing down my short beard. It made me so happy once I could start growing more facial hair, as it made me feel more like a bear. Still a cub, though. I know no matter how old I get I'm sure I'll always want that special someone to look after me.

It warms my heart to think that's what Beckett had with his Shawn.

He opened up a bit more about his late husband over dinner, telling me cute stories and just generally reminiscing about their love. He was only a few years younger than Beckett, but they sound to have had the kind of relationship dynamic I think I'd be looking for long term.

There's always a moment when I wrestle with myself whether or not I'm being selfish by wanting to be doted on. But apparently, that's quite a common worry for people like me. The important thing to remember is that as much as I want to be taken care of, there are people out there like Beckett who thrive on doing the caretaking as well. Gardens and gardeners. Subs and Doms. Boys and Daddies. All of those roles are okay—wonderful, even—if everyone knows where they stand.

Unlike with Mick last night.

I shudder as I think how badly wrong my night could have gone if Beckett hadn't been there. I hope that I wouldn't have allowed myself to be pressured into anything I didn't want. But even if I'd managed to get myself out of that mess, I probably would have fled to my room, cried the whole night, then left to go home this morning.

Instead, I'm on my way to meet Beckett for breakfast, and then we're going to explore one of the nature trails.

And now I really am late. I grab my keycard and rush out the door, taking a second to make sure it's definitely locked before flying down the stairs and rushing out of the building.

Holy fuck.

It's *so* much colder than it was yesterday. What happened? Well, I don't have a hat, gloves, or even a scarf, so there's no point in going back to my room. I decide to jog all the way to the main lodge, and that warms me up quite nicely. I'm a little worried about going for this walk now, but perhaps coffee will heat me up from the inside.

The dining hall is pretty crowded. I scan the couple dozen faces, but Beckett is quite easy to spot. He's got a table for two, and he smiles as we catch each other's eyes, beckoning me over to join him. Unfortunately, I also see Mick, but thankfully, he doesn't notice me. He appears to be too busy grumbling to another surly-looking Daddy. I realize that Beckett has secured us a table as far away from them as possible, and I let out a breath of relief.

"Hi," I say cheerfully as I approach the empty seat opposite him. "I'm sorry I'm late."

"You're right on time," he assures me kindly. "But you're a little underdressed. You know there's a storm blowing in this afternoon, right?"

I still just as I take my seat. "No?" I say nervously. I never checked the weather, though. I just assumed. We're close enough to home that I figured I knew what the conditions would be this time of year without thinking about looking it up.

Beckett just smiles, however. "Not to worry. I've got a spare scarf and such that I keep in my car. You can borrow those for our walk, if you'd like?"

I know he just wants to keep me warm, which in itself is pretty awesome. But the idea that I'll be wearing something of his makes my heart flip.

"Oh, thank you. That's so kind."

"Not at all," he says. "Why don't you head up to the buffet and get some breakfast? I'm all right with this tea for now."

Of course he's drinking tea instead of coffee. How British of him. "Can I get you anything while I'm up?" I offer. I still feel all warm and fuzzy from how he sorted dinner for us last night, and I'd like to return the favor if I can.

He beams at me. "I'll certainly take some pancakes and bacon with maple syrup," he says.

I can't help but laugh. "That's so American."

He grins. "What can I say? I've been assimilated."

I happily trot up to the food carts and load up with two plates of bacon, pancakes, and some hash browns for good measure. Then I get some coffee from the machine with plenty of milk and sugar.

I manage to get everything back to our table, and love how Beckett smiles at me. I know I want him to Daddy me, but I also want to show my appreciation back to him.

"Thank you so much," he says.

The food is just as delicious as last night. I thought a small place like this in the middle of nowhere might be a bit crap. But they've obviously got a good chef working for them, and I very much enjoy my breakfast. If we're going to go out walking in the cold, loading up on carbs seems like a sensible idea.

"Did you sleep well?" Beckett asks once we're not quite so ravenous.

I try not to blush. It's an innocent question. But the truth is I did sleep well. Like a log, in fact.

And I dreamed of him.

A very not-safe-for-work dream that I had to 'sort out' once I woke up. Obviously, I'm not going to tell him that, but my memories threaten to betray me.

"Uh, yeah," I say, covering up some of my face with my mug of coffee in case I'm blushing. "The pillows are nice."

We end up having a silly little chat about pillow preferences and thread counts. It's hardly scintillating, but I kind of love it for its domesticity. I just have the same twin bed I've always had at home, but he describes how his king has a ton of throw pillows and extra blankets and stuff.

"I hate being cold," he admits. "It's always better to be cozy, I feel."

I couldn't agree more.

Once we're done, we head outside to Beckett's car. He's got a big black Jeep that's so shiny and new compared to my beat-up wreck. I don't point it out to him in the lot, and am grateful he doesn't ask.

"Here we go," he says triumphantly as he pulls out a matching set of purple gloves, hat, and scarf from the back pocket on the passenger seat. "I've had those there in case of emergency for years. It feels good to finally use them."

I see he's also got a box of tissues, a pack of wooden cutlery, an ice scraper, a phone charger, an umbrella, and a bunch of other stuff sticking out of the two pockets behind the seats. My car doesn't have any of those things, but I suppose it really should.

If I had a Daddy, I bet he'd make sure I was properly kitted out.

"Thank you," I say gratefully, going to take the items from him. He does hand over the hat and gloves, but I freeze as he carefully wraps the scarf around my neck himself.

"There we are," he says proudly, stepping back to admire his work. I definitely blush this time and hastily jam the hat on my head before pulling the gloves on.

"That's much better, thanks," I say, hoping I sound casual and not like a lovesick puppy. I know this is just an infatuation, but damn it's hard to stop the tremble from coming out in my voice. He's just so perfect he makes my knees weak.

However, nothing's going to happen today. It doesn't matter how badly these feelings are growing like some sort of out-of-control science experiment. I promised to respect his boundaries, and I'm not breaking my word on that.

I can't help but nurture a tiny hope, though. We've swapped numbers and he lives in Chicago. My town, Alder, is in the suburbs. This doesn't have to be make or break this weekend. We can keep in touch, and maybe something might slowly develop.

I know I've gotten myself in so much trouble lately from jumping into things too fast, but I can't help but feel strongly that Beckett is drawn to me as well. Otherwise, why would he want to spend all this time with me and give me his scarf and stuff? I'm sure I'm not imagining it. And actually, fantasizing about a slow-burn romance in the future is kind of the opposite of jumping the gun, right?

We're quiet as we head away from the main lodge onto one of the signposted trails that leads into the forest. Beckett mentioned over breakfast that he thought we should do the shortest, easiest one just in case the weather turns on us, and I'm glad we made that choice now. The sky has gone from yesterday's periwinkle blue to a purplish gray. Luckily, the trees are shielding us from the majority of the wind.

I hope it clears up by tomorrow. I'm a pretty good driver, but I'm terrified of extreme weather conditions. What if it doesn't? Beckett's app said it could get worse before it gets better at the start of next week. I can't miss work. Or worse —what if I get stranded on the roadside in a blizzard?

A lightbulb goes off in my head.

What if I can solve both of my problems at once?

I'm that worried about wrecking things with Beckett by giving in to temptation, so what if I remove myself from the situation? If I'm hoping we can connect again after this retreat, what does it matter when I leave? It only matters that I don't ruin anything.

So why don't I leave now, before the storm and before I say or do anything I'll regret?

I glance at Beckett. The idea of leaving him this soon pains me. But now that the thought has been planted in my head, I think it's the right thing to do.

I'll just have to hope this is the beginning of something amazing and not the end before we've even started.

CHAPTER 7

Beckett

My first thought is that this has got to be my fault. I tried so hard not to send mixed messages, but it's not surprising that I've managed to fuck things up.

I told Laurie that I wanted to go slow, but then I went and became completely infatuated with him literally overnight.

I'm a terrible person.

"You're leaving?" I repeat faintly.

"Oh, um, yeah," he says cheerfully from across the dining table.

After our walk, I'd suggested we grab lunch and then have a go at some of the afternoon activities together. In retrospect, I did notice how quiet he was outside, but I was determined that if I just took care of him well enough, he'd come back out of his shell again. I should have given him some bloody space.

"It's okay," he says reassuringly, then gives me a cute smile. It doesn't quite reach his eyes, though, so I'm worried things aren't really okay. "I had no idea about the storm, and I just think I'll feel much better if I get out ahead of it instead of waiting until tomorrow. I'm a bit of an anxious driver."

I glance nervously toward the windows. This thing is coming in hard and fast. My weather app is changing by the hour, and now it's predicting snow and a lot of it. I don't like the idea of Laurie being caught out in it at all, so maybe he's right to try and beat it.

Except I just want to keep him here where I know he's safe.

"Of course," I say, trying to put on a brave face for him. I fear, however, after the past couple of years, I've gotten completely out of practice. I stopped trying to school my emotions after I lost Shawn. Bottling them up would have made me explode. So I'm not surprised when Laurie's expression becomes concerned.

"It's not you," he blurts. Then he blushes adorably like he's done several times since we met. I like how he wears his heart on his sleeve.

"Well, I'm very glad to hear that," I say, equally trying to be honest without overwhelming him.

He bites his lip and looks at me with those pretty green eyes. "Maybe when you get back home, you could, um, drop me a text. Only if you feel like it, I mean. I don't want to pressure you or anything."

My heart aches. He's worrying about me, and I'm worrying about him. I have to smile. It's all rather adorable.

I take a deep breath and hold out my hand—the left one so my wedding ring glints under the dining hall lights. I like to think of it as Shawn winking at me, telling me to get my head out of my arse.

His face lights up, and he slips his palm against mine. "I would be very interested in staying in touch," I say sincerely. "You're a special young man, Laurie. I'd be lying if I said I wasn't disappointed that our time is going to be cut short this weekend, but your well-being is extremely important to me. If you want to head off now and try and beat the storm, I completely understand." I chuckle ruefully. "I wish I could drive you back myself, but there's the little matter of what would happen to your car."

He lets out a laugh too and beams at me. "You'd really drive me home?"

I raise my eyebrows. "If it meant getting to spend another day with you? Yes, absolutely. But I totally get why you want to depart early, so please don't feel bad."

He smiles and fiddles his fingers against mine. "If we can stay in touch, then I don't mind having to leave now. Well, not as much," he adds, a sparkle in his eyes.

"I would really love to stay in touch," I tell him earnestly.

Oh, yes. There's no way I'm letting this one slip out of my life. In fact, the thought of it makes my chest tighten and my throat thicken. It's almost like I feel Shawn's hands squeeze my shoulders, telling me to calm down.

This time yesterday, I didn't even want to come here and was determined that no boy or cub could possibly entice me into anything. It still felt far too soon to even consider replacing Shawn.

But that phantom squeeze comes again on my shoulders, like the ghost of my late husband is urging me not to blow this.

So which is it? Have I come on too strong or not enough? Or is Laurie really just that worried about the weather that he wants to take off from the getaway early?

God, I am out of practice at being with someone. I used to be so good, it just came as naturally as breathing. But…that's it, isn't it? It just needs to be natural. The only thing I have to worry about is his health and happiness, and everything else will fall into place. He seems genuinely eager to stay in touch, so even if I have influenced his leaving early, I can't have fucked anything up *that* badly.

Right, what does he need from me? What would I do if I were his Daddy?

"Okay, so do you have gas?" I start by asking him. There, that's something nice and solid that I can manage. It doesn't have to get all tangled up in too many feelings. By anticipating any troubles he might have on his journey, I can keep things simple.

He nibbles his lower lip as he thinks. "I might have been getting low, actually. But there was a gas station that I passed about fifteen minutes before I got here, so I can head straight there."

"Good," I say with a nod, starting to feel mollified. "Make sure you have a bottle of water. You can take the complimentary one from your room. And I'd like you to keep the hat, gloves, and scarf I gave you."

His eyes go wide like saucers, and for a second, I worry that I've overstepped. But then he whispers, "Really?" and I think I understand how much that means to him.

My heart swells to twice its size.

"Of course," I say gently, rubbing the back of his hand with my thumb. "You can give them back to me when we next meet up."

I don't really care about getting them back. I bought them specifically for the car, and they don't have any sentimental value to me. What I wanted to do was assure him that I fully intend on making sure we meet up again.

I have a feeling part of his leaving is to give me space, and honestly, that's probably the most sensible thing either of us has done since I caught him midfall on the front steps. A little time and distance will ensure both of us aren't rushing into anything.

But I know with my whole heart that I want to see him again *sometime*, even if that's next week or six months from now.

"I'll look after them," he promises.

I squeeze his hand. "Thank you, but I want you to look after yourself far more," I assure him. "Now, if you're going to beat this storm, we better get you on your way sooner rather than later."

He swallows, and doubt flickers across his face. "Will you be all right?"

I grin, finding his concern so lovable. It warms my heart. I've never had any interest in anyone who just wants to take, not give, in a relationship. I might want to dote on him, but I would never be attracted to anyone who was selfish and thoughtless at their core.

"Oh, that Jeep can handle pretty much anything," I tell him.

I don't want to make him feel bad or put any pressure on him, but I'm pretty sure the worst of the storm will blow over by the time I'm due to leave on Monday morning. And to be honest, if I *am* detained, I have so much unused holiday at my disposal, taking a spontaneous day or two if I need it won't be any big deal.

He looks around, possibly thinking that other people don't look panicked. They might be thinking the same as me, or they might be completely oblivious to the situation. I know not everyone keeps a sharp eye on the weather. It's just a habit I've always had.

But whatever the reason, Laurie shouldn't be worrying about them. If he's an anxious driver, then he needs to do what's best for him and not concern himself with anyone else.

"I'll text you as soon as I'm home," I promise him. "So long as you do the same tonight?"

He relaxes and smiles at me. "Absolutely," he promises.

"All right," I say, realizing I need to stop delaying the

inevitable. "Let me walk you to your room. I imagine it won't take you long to pack."

He shakes his head as we both rise to our feet. "It's always so much easier packing to go home than to go on vacation, isn't it? I suppose because you don't have to make any decisions. You just have to shove everything back into the bag it came from."

I marvel at his sweet innocence. I love how earnest and excited he is about things I've been taking for granted. He makes me feel like I'm seeing the world through fresh eyes again.

The walk back to his building isn't long enough, but I know I need to give him that space now that I was worried I didn't give him earlier. As much as I want to Daddy him, he is an adult, and he's made a decision. I have to respect that and walk away before I put my foot in it and muck this relationship up before it's even had a chance to bloom.

"It's been utterly charming to meet you, Laurie," I say as we stop at the front door. I slip my hands into my coat pockets and rock on my feet, trying not to be awkward, but it's just been so long since my heart felt awake. I'm not sure the best way to handle things anymore, especially in these perilous uncharted waters.

Laurie hugs himself and looks sweetly at me. He's not much shorter than me, and he's definitely got a thicker frame, but in that moment, he looks so delicate and small. It makes my heart ache.

"It was great meeting you, too," he says shyly.

I can't hold back. I pull my hands out of my pockets and step forward to wrap my arms around him. He immediately melts into the embrace and sighs, tucking his face against my neck. I rub his back and appreciate the clean ocean scent he's wearing. I love the soft feel of his beard in comparison to my shorter stubble that's grown since yesterday.

I haven't felt like this since I met Shawn.

Like a puzzle piece locking together with its perfect neighbor. But I suppose that's the thing about puzzle pieces. They have more than one side. They can fit together in more than one way.

We naturally part, and there's a moment when it feels like we could easily lean in and kiss. But I make an executive decision and step backward, not wanting to rush into anything.

"Text me when you get home," I remind him, managing to keep my voice under control when it could have easily shaken with emotion.

"I will," he promises.

Before the pause can stretch out and get uncomfortable, I raise my hand in a short wave, then turn and walk away. I take a deep breath of cold air, exhaling and walking through the cloud of condensation that forms.

"It's going to be okay," I tell myself.

Because it has to be.

CHAPTER 8

Laurie

MY MIND THINKS I'VE DONE THE RIGHT THING.

My heart thinks my brain is talking out of my ass.

I am in such a state it takes me three times as long as it should to pack up my room at the lodge. I keep sniffling and choking up, wondering if I'm making a huge mistake. I almost run out to find Beckett several times. I keep imagining him meeting someone else here at the retreat once I've gone. I know that's incredibly unlikely, as he said he's not interested in looking for anyone right now.

But he met me.

Eventually, I manage to get my shit together (literally and figuratively) and leave my empty room behind. The bear cub behind the desk seems thrilled that they've suddenly got another room available, and happily gives me a refund, even though it's so last minute.

"The storm is scaring folks off the road," he says, shaking his head as he puts the money back on my card. I notice his name tag says 'Billy.' "You stay safe now."

"Thanks," I say weakly, taking the card back and wondering for the hundredth time if I'm completely fucking everything up. But I keep coming back to the idea that I can't get stranded here, and it will actually be the best for me and Beckett if one of us goes. I want to give this relationship the best chance I can, so I stick to the plan and head back outside.

In the time I've been packing and checking out, the sky has gone from purple to iron gray. The wind is howling and there's already a decent dusting of snow over everything. I shiver, grateful for Beckett's gloves, hat, and scarf.

I don't have time to think. I have to get a move on. I've seen how fast snowstorms can cause havoc, and I have no intention of getting caught up in this one. Damn it. If I wasn't so lovesick, I could have realized the danger earlier and gotten myself out of here faster. Well, I guess there's no point in dwelling on that now. The best thing I can do is get in the car and put my foot down.

My heart sinks, though, when I turn the ignition and see what my situation actually is. I must have been distracted when I arrived, as I didn't remember how low on gas I actually am.

"Okay," I say to myself out loud, eyeing up the needle. "We're not completely screwed."

I *should* be able to make it to the gas station, but there's absolutely no way in hell I can save time by skipping that and heading straight home. That's okay, though. I can be fast. And the refund I just got back from the hotel room means I'll be less anxious than usual about getting a full tank. I think that it will be sensible to stock up right now.

All right, that's enough of a plan for me to throw my crappy car into drive and pull out of the parking lot. As worried as I am, I do take a moment to glance in the rearview mirror and feel a pang as I leave Shellridge Lodge behind.

I'd been so looking forward to this trip, and it's already

over. I'd been excited to meet Pancake Papa, and it turned out I met someone a million times better than him. I know I'm doing what's best for me by trying to beat the snow, but I do also allow myself a moment to be sad.

Soon, though, I'm too distracted to think about much else than the road and staying on it. The snow is flinging down to the ground, and I'm trying to remember every trick I've been taught about how to best navigate it as I slowly crawl into the gas station.

I jam the pump into my car as fast as possible, shivering violently as the wind cuts through me. It feels like it takes forever as I watch the amount slowly ticking upward, but finally, mercifully, it hits the number where I know the tank will be mostly full. So I disconnect and pay quickly with my card, eager to get back on the road.

Knowing I have fuel does make me feel slightly better, but I'm still a bag of nerves as I pull onto the road once again. I'll be happier once I get to Route 47, but on this twisting back road, there are hardly any cars, and it definitely hasn't been salted. I can feel the steering wheel fighting me every now and again, and I have to remind myself to breathe as I creep along in the thick snow.

I'm torn between wanting to take it slow so I can be as careful as possible and flooring it so I can just get home and leave all this stress behind me. My heart is hammering, and my mouth is dry. I notice that I never picked up the bottle of water like Beckett told me to. I could have grabbed something at the gas station if I'd realized, damn it. Okay, I can manage a little longer without a drink. I just need to get to the freeway, and then it'll be plain sailing all the way back to Alder.

There's no warning.

One moment, I'm forging my way along the road, concentrating extra hard on making sure I'm still on the correct side as I can't see the markings anymore. The next, the car is sliding violently to the left across the other lane. I yell and slam my foot on the brake—exactly what you're not supposed to do. The car swivels and careens into the edge of the woods that flank the road, smashing between a few trees and tilting for a heart-stopping second.

"No, no, *no!*" I cry as gravity betrays me, and the car tips on its side. I hear my suitcase slam down in the trunk, and my whole body suddenly is pulling against the seat belt. The car is still somehow bouncing between the trees farther into the woods. A window breaks, and glass rains down around me. I realize I'm screaming. I'm practically lying on the driver's door, and the window is a cracked mess. I'm still gripping the wheel like that might do anything to help me at this point.

Eventually, the car comes to an abrupt halt, flinging me forward. Then everything is eerily still and quiet.

I gasp for air, shaking from head to toe, my head swimming. It's over. I've stopped.

Now what?

I pat myself down and am pretty sure nothing is broken, and I don't seem to be bleeding heavily. I can feel a few little cuts from the glass that shattered around me, but honestly, I'm so numb from the shock and cold right now, and I can barely feel them.

"Get out of the car," I utter to myself, speaking out loud in an attempt to jolt myself into action. I fumble with the seatbelt clasp until I can free myself. The car is still on its side, and I gulp as I look up at the windowless passenger side door that's facing the dark sky. The trees are offering some protection, but there are still thick snowflakes drifting inside and landing on me.

Okay. I guess I have to climb. What if the car tips again when I shift my weight? Oh, god. I don't want to have survived this far and then go and hurt myself just trying to get out. I take a second to look around, trying to slow my frantic breathing.

Then I see the front windscreen.

It's got a branch sticking through in the top corner, and the rest of it is a huge spiderweb of cracked glass. I look between it and the empty window above me, weighing up my options.

Climbing seems too risky.

I shift in my seat, getting my legs up and lying more on the driver's door so I can get my lower body above the steering wheel and the dash.

Then I start to kick.

To my immense relief, the entire frame of the windscreen begins to shift. After another thirty seconds of pounding my feet against the reinforced glass, the whole thing gives way, giving me the exit I need.

A sob escapes my throat, and I awkwardly crawl my way to freedom. I can feel little bites from glass and forest debris, but Beckett's gloves protect me a fair bit. I'm sweating and trembling by the time I get out. My head is light and my vision dizzy. But I'm out. Next, I hurry around the back and manage to get the trunk open so I can retrieve my suitcase. It's not until I stumble back to the road and make sure it's a safe distance from the wreck that I burst into tears.

I cling to a tree and try and stop my legs from giving out from under me. But I'm terrified. I'm stranded in a snow-storm. My car is totaled, and I haven't seen another vehicle go past since I got back to the road. I'm not sure it's safe to hang around here, anyway. Another car could hit the same patch of ice or whatever it was that I did and come hurtling straight toward me.

I take a second to wipe my face, the tears freezing against

my skin, then grab my case and move several feet up and use a particularly large tree to shelter behind.

What now?

My shaking hand is already reaching into my pocket, where my phone was mercifully secured. I pull it out and take one of my gloves off so I can unlock it with my finger-print. Then I go immediately to my phonebook and the most recently dialed number.

Beckett.

I manage to keep it together as it starts to ring, thankful I even have a signal out here. But as soon as the call goes through, I lose what little composure I had left.

"Laurie?" Beckett answers, the concern clear in his voice.

"Daddy!" I cry out.

CHAPTER 9
Beckett

THAT ONE WORD SHATTERS MY ENTIRE WORLD.

"Sweetheart, what's happened?" I cry, jumping up from my seat at the back of the life drawing class, not caring that everyone turns to stare. I wasn't particularly invested in the activity anyway. I was just trying to distract myself from the ache I felt in my heart from Laurie's absence. I'm so incredibly relieved I had my phone out so I wouldn't miss a call, even though it's set to silent.

Something has clearly happened, and my only concern now is finding out what that is and fixing it.

"My car came off the road," he sobs, and my heart cracks at his anguish. "It flipped on its side, and I don't know what to do—"

"Whoa, whoa," I say, already running to my car, thankful I had my coat with me in the class. "It's okay, darling. First things first, I need to know if you're all right."

He sniffles for a moment. "I don't think I'm hurt," he says quietly. "But I'm so cold."

I bite my tongue to stop myself from shouting at the sky for daring to put my sweet boy in danger. Instead, I sprint the last several meters across the parking lot and unlock the door as fast as I can.

"I know, baby. You're being so brave. It's okay now, I promise. Just tell me where you are, and I'll come get you. Were there any other cars involved? Is there a danger to other drivers?"

I realize I've bombarded him a bit, but he takes a shaky breath and starts talking. "No other cars, no. I think I hit black ice or slush or something, so another driver could do the same, but my car is completely off the road. And I'm not sure exactly where I am, but I'm on the only road that leads south to the highway. A few cars have gone past, but I didn't want to endanger anyone else by flagging them down."

"Good boy," I say emphatically. I put the phone on speaker and mount it on my dash, barely getting my belt fastened before spinning the wheels and tearing out of the lot. "You did the right thing. I'm not going to leave you, okay? I'll stay on the phone until I find you. We can worry about calling the police and getting your car towed once the storm passes. Right now, we just need to get you back where it's safe and warm, all right?"

"Yes, Beckett," he says quietly. I imagine his adrenaline will be wearing off, and shock will be setting in, not to mention how freezing he must be. The snow is so thick it feels like night has already fallen, even though it's still only the afternoon. I flick the heated seats on and crank up the hot air in anticipation of getting him in here, then press on the gas pedal a little harder.

I honestly bought a Jeep because I had one back home, where there were a lot more country roads. I rarely need four-wheel drive out here in Illinois, but right now, I'm incredibly grateful for it. I feel far more confident than I would in a regular car.

However, I'm bitterly regretting ever letting Laurie leave.

I knew this storm was coming in fast, but I didn't want to smother or overwhelm him. Now we've ended up in this mess. He must have been so terrified if his car flipped like he said it did. I'd give anything to have avoided that for him. But I know better than anyone that there's no sense in gnashing my teeth about the past and what could have been. The only thing I can do now is be present in this moment and do everything I can to help the sweet boy I've taken under my wing.

That doesn't mean I'm done blaming myself, though.

"Fucking idiot," I mutter crossly to myself. Laurie is okay, and soon he'll be back with me and there's no way in hell I'll be letting him out of my sight until every single snowflake has melted.

"Beckett?" Laurie says, and I realize he heard me talking to myself.

"Sorry, sweet boy," I say. "Can you tell me how long after the gas station it was that you came off the road?"

"Um…I'm not sure. Maybe five minutes?"

"Right, fantastic. I'm just going past it now, all right? I want you to make sure you're safe, but if you can keep an eye on the road and watch out for me, I should be there soon."

"Okay, Beckett," he says in a trembling voice.

I'm terrified of missing him in the snow, but he must spot me first because when I finally see him, he's waving his arms to get my attention. My heart leaps into my throat as I slow down and end the phone call. There aren't any other vehicles around that I can tell—they're probably sensibly staying home. But I'm still extremely careful as I pull off the road and yank the handbrake on, leaving the engine running as I throw off my seatbelt and jump from the car.

My heart might have cracked before, but it clean breaks in two as I see Laurie burst into tears and run toward me. I fling my arms around him and hug him tightly to me.

"It's okay," I tell him. "It's okay. Daddy's here. You're all right."

I've said it now. The D-word. I know I promised myself I wouldn't rush into anything, but every fiber of my being has to Daddy him right now in this moment. And that's nothing compared to the gut-wrenching horror I experience as I look over his shoulder and see the twisted wreckage of his car.

Jesus fucking Christ.

It's so clear what could have easily happened. The fact that he got out of that with hardly a scratch makes my blood run far colder than the snow has. Quite frankly, it feels like a miracle.

I know what it's like to be with someone as they slip from this life into the next. I know what it's like to rage and cry and feel so unbelievably cheated of the time we could have had together that was so cruelly taken away. The thought that Laurie could have been snatched away from me in an instant is almost too painful to bear.

"Let's get you warm," I say. He nods against me. I pick up his case and lead him back to the Jeep, opening the door so he can hop inside.

I quickly secure his suitcase inside the back of the car, then rush around to the driver's side. I don't want to linger on this treacherous stretch of road any longer than we have to. I do take a second to mark the location on my phone, though, so we can more easily find his car again if we need to lead the proper authorities this way.

"It all happened so fast," Laurie says, looking out the window at his car and sounding stunned. I reach over and take his gloved hand, grateful that I left the engine running and the warm air blowing. He's already looking less like a human Popsicle. Carefully, I do a three-point turn to get us facing the right direction, and head off. "I guess my dad almost got his wish."

I frown, not following what he's saying at all. "His wish?"

Laurie shrugs, his expression taut as he stares out of the window in front of him. "For me to be killed in a car crash."

"Sweet boy, no!" I cry in horror. I have to keep my eyes on the road, but I squeeze his hand harder and glance over at him as much as I can. "You shouldn't be thinking about him or that, okay? Fuck him. This was just an accident, and I'm just so relieved that you're unhurt."

That doesn't convey a tenth of the emotion I'm feeling, but I'm concerned that if I open up the floodgates, they won't close again, and I need to get us home. If I allow myself to be as furious as I want at his shithead of a father, I'll run my car off the road as well, which would be a complete disaster. All that matters now is getting Laurie back where it's safe and warm.

He swallows and turns his reddened eyes to look at me. "I can't believe you came out to get me."

I'm not sure what emotion surges through me, but it's some kind of chilled revulsion or disbelief. "Of *course* I came to get you!" I hiss in abhorrence. "Who wouldn't?"

His smile is kind of sad, but he gives me the tiniest laugh as well. "I doubt Mick would have dropped everything and run out into the snow, Beckett."

I scoff. Unfortunately, that's probably very true.

"I'm just so thankful you were able to call me. Let's get off this road and back to where it's safe and warm."

"I like the heated seat," he admits shyly, and I grin over at him before flicking his up a setting. I hate the idea of him being out in this storm for even a minute. He's going to be sweltering by the time I'm finished with him this evening. Only toasty warm bear cubs here.

The storm has possibly gotten worse, and even I feel apprehensive as I crawl back the way we came. I notice in the time I've been collecting Laurie that the gas station has shut up shop. I guess no one's out getting gas anyway, and any employees probably want to get home safe as well.

It's eerie being the only car on the road. Apart from the lodge, though, there isn't much else out here. I'm just thankful we have shelter at all, and I imagine Shellridge will be well stocked so we and all the guests can hunker down until the storm passes.

I'm surprised to see that the parking lot is more packed than when I left it. I figure, though, that if anyone was around here when the storm hit so fast, this would be the most sensible place to come.

"I checked out of my room," Laurie says, breaking my chain of thought.

I find a parking slot and kill the engine before replying. "It's fine. We can get you another one."

"But I spent all that money on gas," he squeaks, visibly starting to get stressed. "Then I immediately crashed my car. I wasted it all!"

I've already got my seatbelt off, so it's easy to turn around and cup either side of his face and encourage him to look at me. "That's not a problem," I say firmly. "We'll sort something out. The only thing that matters is that you're unharmed. Everything else we can tackle as it comes."

He takes a deep breath, then nods. "Thank you," he says. "For everything."

I brush his cheeks with my gloved thumbs, then release his face. "You're more than welcome, sweet boy."

We exit the Jeep into the howling wind and battle to get his suitcase out before slogging it up to the main entrance of the lodge. When I first arrived, I thought it would look so idyllic covered in snow.

Now I'm not so sure.

The lobby is crowded, and I feel my eyebrows rise as Laurie and I step inside. I quickly shut the door to keep the wind out, but there's still a dreadful draft that people are trying to stay out of the way of. Plenty of them are standing but a lot are sitting as well, looking weary. Goodness—are they all sheltering from the storm?

I've got Laurie's suitcase in one hand, and with the other, I grip his reassuringly and push ahead toward the check-in desk. The usually bubbly boy—Billy—gives me a tired look, then his eyes light up.

"You! You're part of the retreat, aren't you? You already have a room." He sounds very relieved.

"Yes," I confirm, then look at Laurie. "But my friend needs one, too. His car ran off the road."

The cub's face falls. "I remember checking you out a little while ago. That's so scary about your car. Are you all right?"

Laurie manages a little smile. "I'm okay, thanks. Shaken, but Beckett came to my rescue."

Billy grins, happy once again. "That's what Daddies are for," he says proudly.

Neither Laurie nor I correct him, and my heart sings.

"I'm afraid it's bad news about the room, though," Billy says, sounding genuinely apologetic. "We're fully booked from walk-ins out of the storm. Daddy is trying to rustle up enough blankets and things for people to camp out in the lounge and here in the lobby where we have sofas and stuff."

I love how casually he called his partner 'Daddy' in front of us. Heather's right—times are changing. But what he said after that leaves us with a problem.

"Oh, it's okay," Laurie says cheerfully. "I'm so incredibly grateful to be out of the storm and not hurt. I'll make do anywhere."

The solution is obvious. My only hesitation is that I didn't want to move too fast or put any further pressure on him. But I just saw how close I came to losing him, and I very quickly decide that life is too bloody short to keep messing around.

"You can stay with me," I say, raising my eyebrows at him, seeing what he thinks of the suggestion. "If you'd like?"

His mouth drops open. "Really?"

"Of course," I say with a nod, then glance at the bear cub. "I can do that, can't I? It's not breaking any fire safety rules or anything?"

Billy appears to have hearts in his eyes and is clutching his hands to his chest. "Of course you can share," he whispers, then he looks specifically at Laurie. "You have a great Daddy."

Laurie bites his lip and glances at me. "I do," he says softly.

CHAPTER 10

Laurie

DESPITE ALL THE BUSTLING CHAOS AROUND US, I SUDDENLY feel like it's just me and Beckett in the whole world. Something crackles between us as we look at each other in front of the check-in desk. I feel like in the last few moments, we've opened Pandora's box.

I heard him call himself Daddy on the roadside. I just didn't know how best to respond to it when I was falling to pieces after the accident. During the drive back to the lodge, I decided to wait for a good moment and try calling him that as well to see how he'd react. But the cute bear cub Billy did it for me, and now Beckett is looking at me like I'm the only thing that matters in the whole world.

Could he be my Daddy?

"Here's a second room key," Billy says, breaking through my trance.

He slides the card across the desk, his eyes bright as he bites his lip, looking like a human wibble emoji. My heart skips a beat. I know all that matters is what Beckett feels. But if this near stranger is shipping us, it gives me a flicker of hope.

"Thank you," I say, taking it and slipping it into my pocket.

"You guys take care and stay warm now," he says, something devilish sparkling in his eyes. I blush and glance at Beckett, but he just beams at me. When he looks at me like that, I feel like I'm being thawed from the inside out.

"We will," he tells the cub, and we move away from the desk to make way for someone else who's apparently also just come in from the storm looking for shelter.

I love how Beckett has carried my small suitcase since he picked me up. It feels like there was never a question he would. That's just part of his job now, and it makes me feel so seen and cherished.

It's a short walk outside to his chalet, but it feels like crossing the Antarctic. It's insane how fast the weather changed.

How fast everything has changed, actually.

We don't say anything as he lets us inside and hastily closes the door behind us. We stamp the slush from our boots and shake off the snow. Then in a blur, he has his arms around me, hugging me tightly, and to my horror, I realize he's trembling.

"I could have lost you," he says, his voice muffled against my scarf.

I cling to him and rub his back through his coat. I love his spicy, woodsy scent. He smells like cedar trees and toasted marshmallows. Being with him feels like a cozy campfire. I hate that he's upset. After everything he went through with his husband, he doesn't deserve any more terrible shocks in this life.

"I'm fine," I assure him. "I'm right here. Everything's okay."

He leans back to look at me, his eyes searching. Wordlessly, he pulls off his gloves, hat, and scarf, dropping them on the dresser closest to us. He then shucks off his coat, hanging it over a chair before coming back to me.

I watch him as he carefully plucks his hat from my head. One by one, he lifts my wrists and peels off the gloves, tugging at each finger until they come loose. He turns my hands, inspecting my palms and knuckles, where I have several little scratches. He rubs his thumb gently over the blemishes. Then he checks my face, where I know from looking in the mirror in the car's sun visor that I just have one small cut on my cheek. It's stinging a bit now that we're back in the warm, but it's not too bad.

Especially when Beckett leans forward and very carefully kisses it.

I gasp, the quiet noise feeling enormous in the otherwise silent room. One of the walls has floor-to-ceiling windows, and the falling snow outside looks almost peaceful from here, where we're safe. But other than that, nothing moves aside from Beckett, and I'm the only thing making any sound.

He doesn't look me in the eye as he moves away again and starts to unwind the scarf he gave me from my neck. He disposes of all those items with his own on the dresser, then he unzips my coat and slides it off my shoulders. My heart is racing in my chest, banging against my ribcage as I try not to move in case I spook him. It's silly, but I feel like what's happening is extremely fragile and precious.

Once our outer layers are off, he hugs me again, running his hands over my back and arms.

"Does anything hurt?" he asks me. "Are you injured in any way?"

I take a steadying breath, enjoying resting my head on his shoulder and clinging to his back like he's my life raft. "Just a few sore muscles," I tell him.

But his concern is so endearing I know that this is the moment I've been waiting for.

"I promise I'm okay...Daddy."

It feels like time slows to a crawl as he moves away enough so he can look me in the eyes. I see so much pain there but also tenderness and longing. I want him to know that he's safe with me because he's certainly my safe space at this moment in time.

"It's been so long since I was called that," he says softly. I expected his voice to be thick with emotion, but he sounds more thoughtful.

"Is it okay?" I ask.

He shakes his head and looks at me in wonder. "From you, baby bear, it's utterly beautiful."

My breath catches at the new pet name. I loved being his sweetheart and all the other monikers, but this feels kind of monumental. Like he's telling me he's all in.

If Shawn was his teddy bear, I am beyond honored to be his baby bear.

It feels as inevitable as the dawn as he leans forward and captures my mouth in a kiss filled with a thousand promises. He claims me thoroughly, his fingers digging into my back. *Yes!* I want to be his, all his!

I cling to his shirt, loving the way his strong body feels against mine. All the adrenaline from the car crash comes flooding back to me, getting my blood pumping and my skin tingling. His lips are firm as he kisses me over and over, his tongue sweeping inside my mouth to find mine. I never want this to end, but eventually, I have to come up for air, and I rest my forehead against his as we both pant.

"Was that all right?" he asks.

"I don't know," I say, feeling playful. "Do it again so we can find out."

He drops his head back to laugh, and it's the most beautiful sound in the world. I know my new Daddy will always carry a sadness in his heart, but I want to make him as happy as I possibly can, even if it's only for one night.

"Sweet boy," he murmurs before capturing my mouth again. "I don't know where you came from, but I'm so glad I found you."

"Daddy," I say again, just because I can.

He runs his hands up and down my back as he plunders my mouth. "What do you want, baby bear?"

"Everything," I tell him honestly and desperately.

I tried so hard to walk away from this because I was afraid that pushing too hard would break it. But right now, this small blossoming thing between us feels invincible. I'm done being cautious. Beckett isn't like George or Mick. He's the real deal, and I'm going to hang on to him with all I've got.

He takes my hand, but before we move anywhere, he kisses the knuckles, melting my heart a little more. Then he leads me farther into the chalet that I haven't even had the chance to appreciate yet. There's a huge sectional couch in front of a fireplace, and above that is a TV almost as big as my bedroom wall back home. I spy a little kitchen and a dining room table for four with a wooden chandelier above it, but that's about all I can take in before Beckett is hauling me into the bedroom.

His bedroom.

I guess it's *our* bedroom for the foreseeable future.

It's been made up so nicely by room service I almost feel a bit bad wrecking it. But not so much that I stop myself from sending the throw pillows flying onto the floor as I scramble up the mattress, eagerly waiting for Beckett to join me.

For the briefest second it occurs to me that I really could have died just an hour or so ago. I'm almost delirious now in the aftermath, and I want Beckett to make me feel so alive.

75

We kick our shoes off, and then he drops down next to me so we're side by side and facing each other. He grins as his hand slides over my hip, squeezing it and encouraging me to shuffle a little closer. He cups his other hand under my jaw as we continue making out. I press my hands to his chest, feeling his warm skin through his shirt.

I need more.

My fingers drift to his buttons, and I tentatively start undoing the top one. He moans and kisses me harder, his hand slipping from my face to the top of my own shirt. Excitement fizzes through me like Champagne, eager to pop from the bottle. My cock throbs between my legs, trying to escape the confines of my jeans. It doesn't help when Beckett throws his top leg over mine and presses our groins together. Although it does feel fucking awesome.

"Want you, Daddy," I mumble against his mouth.

"Baby bear," he utters back.

He's got half my shirt undone, and I've managed the same on his. I'm delighted to discover more tattoos lurking beneath as well as a carpet of dark hair over his chest. He's magnificent.

I feel like he appreciates what he's found as well. He gives me a searing kiss as he squeezes my pecs, rubbing his thumbs over my hardening nipples and making me whimper. Then he reaches between us and makes short work of undoing my fly.

"Is this okay?" he asks breathlessly as he strokes me through my cotton boxers.

I cry out and nod my face against his neck. "Yes, Daddy. *Please.*"

There's a flurry of movement, and the next thing I know is both our pants and underwear have been shoved down, and Beckett has our cocks pressed together, his hand wrapped around them as he jerks us off. It's messy, but it's perfect. I groan against his mouth as he kisses me.

"Good boy," he grunts as his hand flies over our lengths. "Good boy, so good."

"Daddy," I whimper. I feel like all my hopes and dreams, all my anger and disappointment, everything I've experienced in the past twenty-four hours is rushing up to greet me. I'm just a powder keg, watching as the spark races up the fuse, getting closer and closer until...

Boom.

I bellow as I start to come, not caring that it's getting on our clothes and the bedsheets. I'm seeing stars as I gasp for air. Beckett kisses my neck as he milks every last drop from me, then starts coming himself. I watch him make a beautiful mess through my lashes as my eyelids droop heavily. The adrenaline drop comes hard and fast, which isn't surprising after everything that's happened today.

It's also not surprising that a sob tries to escape my chest, but then my Daddy is there, hugging me tightly, not caring that we're half-naked or sticky.

He just wants to take care of me.

That's all I want, too. In the whole wide world.

CHAPTER 11
Beckett

I DON'T WANT TO LET HIM GO, BUT WE'RE IN AN uncomfortable mess on the bed. I sigh and press our temples together, a mix of emotions twisting through me.

I want to look after this sweet boy who I care for so much, but it's hard to keep the guilt at bay when I realize this is the first time in over a decade that someone who isn't Shawn has given me an orgasm.

The existential crisis will have to wait. Cold, dried cum is not what anyone wants, let alone two hairy guys. Focusing on physical tasks helps keep my anxieties at bay, anyway. So I kiss his neck, then nuzzle my nose against his cheek.

"Come on, darling," I say, reluctantly sitting. He does the same and groans. "Let's get cleaned up."

"Okay…Daddy," he says tentatively.

I beam at him, trying to reassure him again that the name is okay. I want to be his Daddy—at least for as long as we're here in this lodge for the retreat. This already feels very fast to be falling into something new. I don't want to push anything too far. But hearing him call me that warms little crevasses of my heart I thought had been sealed off forever.

"Good boy," I say, loving how that makes him blush.

We mostly tuck ourselves away and shuffle into the ensuite bathroom where I promptly begin to undress him completely. He giggles, but other than that he just stays still and watches me work. We managed to spurt and smear cum everywhere, which practically speaking is a little annoying, but I can't deny I feel another fizz of excitement playing the moment over again in my head.

It was fucking hot is what it was. Christ, I'd forgotten the passion of not being able to keep your hands off one another. I've got a taste for this gorgeous boy, and I want more.

Not right now, though. Now, I take a clean washcloth and dampen it with warm water before running it over his cock to make sure I wipe up any of the drops our clothes didn't catch. Then I grab one of the huge fluffy bath robes that the lodge has graciously supplied, and help put it on him.

"There we go," I say proudly. It's as if I can physically feel parts of me healing by nourishing the bit of my soul that craves to take care of others.

He grips the lapels of the dressing gown as I rub his shoulders, looking sweetly at me. "Thank you, Daddy," he says more confidently this time. I like that.

Quickly, I divest myself of my clothes. It's not just that they got cum-splattered. They're also cold and damp from the storm. The robes have been on the heated radiator and are deliciously comfortable.

I lead him back to the bed and kiss his forehead.

"Wait here," I tell him before nipping back out into the main body of the chalet to the kitchen area. I fetch us a glass of water each and a packet of cookies from the welcome basket. I'm mindful of Laurie's panic attack yesterday evening regarding sweet treats, but after that car accident and then the unexpected orgasm, he's in danger of crashing hard, and these could help.

He's snuggled up on his side with his head on the pillows and his knees curled up. He smiles at me as I approach the bed, and my heart flips. For now, I just hand him the water and give him a moment to gulp some down. Night is falling, so I switch a lamp on. Then I put my own glass down on the other nightstand as well as the cookies, before getting cozy on the bed, facing him. He's got his hands pressing together under his cheek like a sleeping angel. I'm glad that his pretty green eyes are wide open, though.

"Hi," I say softly.

"Hi," he says back. Then he slips out one of his hands and reaches for my left one. I let him take it. "Are you okay?" he asks.

I nod because I am. I can't deny it's a little complicated, but what in life isn't?

"I'm wonderful," I say honestly. "You're like a ray of sunshine breaking through the rainclouds I've had looming over my head for so long."

He bites his lip and looks down. "I don't know why you think I'm special," he says quietly. "But thank you."

I don't let go of his hand, but I move our connected fingers and use his knuckle to tilt his own chin up to look at me again. "You're one in a million," I assure him. "Believe me. I've met a *lot* of people in my life. Most of them are not as kind or genuine as you are."

"You work for a charity, yeah?" he prompts. I give him a one-armed shrug.

"Now, yes. But before that—before Shawn got ill—I was a lawyer. A big, scary corporate one. It's what brought me to America as my old company has offices all over the world. I have seen some truly awful examples of humanity. I've witnessed the kinds of things money does to people's morals. It warps their brains. I've seen the depraved try and defend murder and other heinous acts. I was so happy when I met Shawn, who just wanted to get up every single day for his kindergartners and help mold them into the best little kids he could."

Laurie rubs his thumb against my wedding band, looking at it thoughtfully. I watch him, holding my breath.

"He sounds like a really great guy," he says softly.

"Would you like to see a photo of him?" I ask cautiously. I don't want to overstep anything, but his eyes go wide, and he nods enthusiastically.

"That would be lovely."

I reluctantly let him go, but a cautious optimism is bubbling in me. It's not hard to find a good photo on my phone. I made a collection of my favorite pictures of Shawn to help with my grief. At first, it hurt too much to look at them, but they've been bringing me comfort for a while now. I find one of him raising a glass of white wine in the sunshine the summer before he got sick. He looks so carefree and full of life.

"Oh," Laurie says as I hand over my mobile. His expression is intense as he studies the image. "He's gorgeous."

I nudge him gently with my shoulder. "Thank you. But so are you."

He shakes his head. "I'm not comparing anything, honestly. But I guess it makes me happy to see that you like bear-types."

I think for a second. "I am attracted to cuddly people who love life and are unapologetically themselves. Perhaps that leans toward a certain physical type, it's true."

He hands the phone back to me and smiles. "If that's how you see me, then that's wonderful. But it did make me feel better about my body type when I realized it had its own subcategory in gay culture and guys were specifically drawn to it. After seeing things like 'NO FATS' in hundreds of dating profiles, Bears-4-U made me feel like a rockstar." He rolls his eyes. "I just kept meeting the wrong guys."

I chuckle sadly. "Yes, no more of that," I tease him gently.

I don't want to presume that I'll be the last new guy he meets for a while. This thing between us might just last the weekend. Who knows? But I *do* want to impress upon him that he's better than that guy Mick or his awful, cheating ex, George.

I draw him into a hug. "You're my baby bear," I remind him, and he hums against me.

"I love that," he admits, making my heart sing.

But then he starts fiddling with my wedding ring again, and I can't help but worry. "Does it bother you?" I ask softly, almost afraid of the answer.

He alleviates my concerns immediately, though. "Oh, no," he says earnestly. "Not at all. I think it's lovely, actually. Like he's here with us in spirit. I hope that isn't weird. I know you said he wanted you to be happy and…well, I hope the time we're spending together is making you at least a little happy."

For a moment, I'm too emotional to speak. I blink a few times and try and swallow. "It's not weird," I manage to say eventually. "That makes me extremely happy to hear. I don't think Shawn will ever fully leave me."

"And he shouldn't have to," Laurie says with a sweet little frown, concentrating on the band again.

But I'm focused on his face. His expressive eyes and his mouth which forms such empathic words.

This boy is incredibly special.

This isn't just lust or grief talking. My heart is doubling in size from simply being around him. I open my mouth to say…I'm not sure what. How I don't want this weekend to end? How I want to stay in touch after we're both back home living our real lives? How I don't think this infatuation with him is going to fade anytime soon? But I don't say any of that.

Because all of the lights suddenly go out, plunging us into darkness.

CHAPTER 12

Laurie

WE'RE ONLY PLUNGED INTO DARKNESS FOR A FEW SECONDS before the lights come back on again, but I know that's still not good.

"What do you think happened?" I whisper as if being too loud might cause the power to go out for good this time.

Beckett shakes his head. "I'm not entirely sure, but I think it might be worth checking." He rolls over and picks up the chalet phone, but then grimaces and puts it back down again. "The line's dead. I think I'll pop over to the main lodge again quickly and see what's what."

"Can I come with you?" I ask, hoping I don't sound too needy.

But Beckett gives me a warm look and reaches over to cup the side of my face. "Of course you can, sweetheart. I just thought you might want to stay in the warmth."

"I want to stay with you," I say.

The conversation we just had resonated hard with me. I need to trust Beckett if I'm going to be with him, as that's never something I truly had with George. For that to work, I need to be open about what I want and need. I'm aware that

84

we haven't known each other long, but he makes me less afraid, to be honest.

He's still got his palm against my cheek as he leans down to kiss me gently. "Then we better get some more clothes on you."

Warmth blossoms in my chest. I know I'm like a puppy who's been told he can come with his master, and some people might find that pathetic. But that's why we work together so well. He wants to give his blessing, and I need to hear it to feel secure.

I watch as he fetches my small suitcase and opens it up. I didn't bother locking it as I wasn't putting it on a plane or anything. He takes stock of the contents, and I'm glad I packed it all neatly.

"Can I make a suggestion?" he asks. I nod. He pulls out a fresh, clean pair of jeans along with a T-shirt, a sweater, and some underwear. There's nothing particularly remarkable about the selection, but my heart is fluttering anyway because *he* picked them. "May I?"

I'm not really sure what he's asking, but seeing as I already trust him so much, I nod in affirmation anyway. I soon find out what he means.

He starts by angling me so I'm sitting on the bed with my feet hanging over the edge. He rolls the socks onto each of my feet before undoing the tie on my robe and encouraging me to stand. He holds out the boxers and gets me to step into them. Even though my cock is by his face, it's soft, and there's nothing particularly sexual between us, although what he's doing is so intimate I feel dizzy with it all.

With my underwear in place, he helps me into my jeans before sliding the robe off down my arms, then assisting me to first put on the T-shirt and then the sweater. He grins and gives my smiling mouth a little kiss.

"Is that all right?"

"It's perfect, Daddy," I assure him. I'm feeling more and more confident every time I say that word, especially seeing how his eyes light up when I use it.

He quickly throws some clothes of his own on—a suit, of course, complete with a vest. I'm almost disappointed he doesn't have a pocket watch. But then he's back over to me, putting on my coat with the gloves, hat, and scarf he's loaned me.

"There we are," he says before kissing the tip of my nose and making me giggle. "All ready to face the elements."

I glance out of the bedroom window at the still raging storm. I'm not sure 'ready' is the correct word, but I loved being dressed by my Daddy, that's for damn sure.

As soon as he's got his own outer layers on, we head out the front door into the dark. It's shockingly cold, and the wind is howling like a wounded wolf, but I think the staff must have salted the main paths because after we fight through the several inches of snow just outside the chalet, the rest of the walk isn't so terrible underfoot to reach the main lodge.

Still, it's a relief once we get inside. I gasp at the warm air and stamp my feet on the already sodden welcome mat at the front entrance, shaking excess snow from my head and shoulders. It's pandemonium. The bear cub, Billy, who I think runs the place with his Daddy, is standing on a chair, waving his arms at the threshold between the lobby and the dining hall. Guests are gathered all around him, clamoring and asking questions, some of them shouting.

"Like I said!" he bellows, throwing up his hands like he's trying to slow down an aircraft. The crowd quietens enough for me to at least hear what he's saying. "The power has gone out. We've lost the phone lines, and cell service isn't great. But our emergency backup generator has kicked in, so we'll have enough heat and electricity for a couple more days, which should be more than enough. However, if we can please ask you to keep energy consumption to a minimum if at all possible, that will help make everything go a little further."

There's a lot of murmuring and nodding. Beckett squeezes me against his side. "There we go," he says with a relieved sigh. "Nothing to worry about."

I mean, I don't think there's *nothing* to worry about. But he's right that for now, we're okay. So long as we still have heat, we're not in any real danger.

Although it seems not everybody feels the same way.

"This is bullshit!" Why am I not surprised that it's Mick who's spoken, shoving his way to the front of the crowd. "You can't tell us what to do! You can't keep us here, either!"

Daddy Bear appears out of nowhere next to his bear cub, Billy, which is pretty impressive considering his size. He folds his arms and glares at Mick, who's so dumb he doesn't back off but bristles even more and tries to get in Daddy Bear's face.

"We're not keeping you here," Daddy Bear rumbles. "But as our guest, we expect you to be courteous of others, and that means conserving energy so the generator lasts as long as possible."

Mick scoffs. "Oh, I'm out of here," he says, throwing up his hands and looking around to sneer at the crowd. "You're all a bunch of pussies. Haven't you ever seen snow before?"

Wow. I wonder what the hell I *ever* saw in that man. I know it was all online until yesterday, but holy shit, he's got so many red flags I could make bunting, for crying out loud.

One guy in a blue flannel shirt rolls his eyes. "I'm Canadian. This isn't that bad. But if you think you can drive on unplowed roads without chains, good luck to you, buddy."

Mick curls his lip at him. "Oh I'll be just fine, don't you

worry. As soon as I hit the gas station, I'll be outta here. This whole event blows, anyway."

I don't know why I do it. I should just let him get on and make his own mistakes. But the good Samaritan in me can't just stand by while he rushes headlong into trouble.

"The gas station is closed," I pipe up. "And the roads definitely aren't salted. I totaled my car just a couple of hours ago, and it's been snowing like crazy ever since."

A lot of people turn my way, most nodding thoughtfully or looking concerned. But not Mick. Of course.

He jabs a finger and stomps several feet toward me. "I wouldn't even *be* here if it wasn't for you, you little prick tease," he snarls. "I come all this way, and you blow me off for some British douchebag!"

Beckett steps between me and Mick before he can get too close. "You ruined that rendezvous all by yourself, remember?" he says pointedly. I'm shaking with my heart in my mouth, but he looks completely calm and collected.

Mick is fuming, though, obviously recalling what Beckett said about informing the organizers of his appalling behavior. "Fine. I'll leave whenever I want to, though. I bet there's some other gas station around that isn't so afraid of a little snow."

"That's the only one for a good ten miles," Daddy Bear says coolly. "So why don't you simmer down and stop making such a ruckus, hmm?"

Mick looks like he wants to continue fighting. But after a few seconds, he apparently comes to his senses and backs off. I release the breath I didn't even know I was holding.

"Whatever. Boss these folks around if it makes you feel all important. I'm no one's prisoner."

He stalks off, many people watching him leave. But then Billy, who's still on the chair, pops a hip and tuts. "*As I was saying before I was so rudely interrupted, we should be fine* for power unless someone decides to throw a midnight rave. If anyone has any questions, please come find us at the check-in desk. If you'd like to stick around, we'll be serving a relaxed buffet-style dinner, so come help yourselves. And don't worry, the one thing we *definitely* won't run out of is booze, so we promise to keep you warm both inside and out!"

That gets a cheer from the crowd, and I smile as well. But I can't deny I'm a little shaken.

Beckett squeezes my side. "Are you okay?"

I shrug. "He's right," I say. "Mick, I mean. He wouldn't be here if it wasn't for me."

Beckett frowns. "I think you'll find, darling boy, that he's a grown man capable of making his own decisions, even if they are very poor ones. Besides, he's not going anywhere. He just wanted to let off steam to show us all how tough he is." Beckett rolls his eyes. "I, for one, am *extremely* glad you made plans to meet him here and that I was then able to save you from those ill-formed plans."

I giggle and relax a little. Maybe Beckett has a point. Mick not only made the decision to come here himself, but he physically can't go anywhere and put himself in danger unless he walks out the front door and tries to get anywhere on foot—which again, will be his own choice. I can't be worrying about him.

I sigh happily and snuggle against Beckett's side. "Shall we get dinner?" I suggest.

He nods enthusiastically. "And I could definitely go for a nice glass of red wine. How about you?"

I hum, actually wanting a drink for the first time this weekend. Beckett makes me that relaxed. "I could go for a white wine spritzer," I say.

Beckett kisses my forehead. "Shawn liked those," he comments.

I feel ridiculously proud. Maybe it might bother other people being compared to someone's late husband, but I take it as an extreme honor.

"Then white wine spritzer it is. Let's enjoy a little bit of normalcy amid all this chaos."

Beckett grins and kisses me on the mouth. "I couldn't have said it better myself. The night is still young, and so are we."

He's right.

And I can't wait to see what the rest of it will turn into.

CHAPTER 13

Beckett

DINNER IS SIMPLE BUT VERY WELCOME. THE KITCHEN STAFF AT Shellridge have made a metric ton of pasta—some of it even gluten-free—with the option of several different sauces. There's also bread, soup, tiramisu, and fresh fruit salad. Laurie and I load up our plates and are lucky enough to find a quiet corner to sit in.

Laurie seems a bit shaken, and I can't blame him. That Mick really is a brute, and he had no right to speak to my baby bear like that. But after several bites of pasta and half a glass of wine and lemonade, he's starting to get the color back in his cheeks.

"Are you all right?" I ask him.

He smiles and scoots his chair a little closer to me, bumping our shoulders together. "Yeah, I'm okay. I don't like anybody being mad at me, but you're right. That's his problem, not mine. I didn't lead him on. It was his crappy personality that drove me away."

"Precisely," I agree, rubbing his back. "You don't need to be worrying about him anymore."

"I'm not, not really," he assures me. "I am a bit concerned

HJ WELCH

about getting back home, though. Do you think they'll get the roads cleared tomorrow if the storm lets up?"

I don't want to add to his troubles, but I'm not going to lie to him either. "I think we might need to brace ourselves for another couple of days here."

He sighs, but then he smiles at me. "At least that gives us more time together."

My heart swells. "Absolutely. But there's something else bothering you?"

He plays with his fork. "I don't like my job, but I am anxious about getting back to it on Monday, yeah. It pays my share of the bills, and I don't want to let my mama down. The company doesn't like us taking unexpected vacation."

I nod in understanding and sympathy. "I get that, but hopefully they won't be too unfair on you if we do get stuck."

He shrugs. "I guess if they fire me, I'll just have to find another crappy job."

I frown, not liking the sound of that. "What would you do if you could do anything?" I ask.

He raises his eyebrows at me. "Honestly? I'd move to the city and take any job I could at any theater. I'd sell popcorn at intermission, I swear. I just want a chance to work my way up doing something like I do now at the community place. I love making theater happen. I think maybe I'd like to try and get into stage management. They're the ones who make sure everything runs properly and that the cast and crew are okay. They take care of the props, cue the show, note down blocking, that sort of thing. I've thought about directing or light design, but I like the sound of management. It feels like they're the ones who bring the community together."

He's glowing by the time he's finished speaking and looks at me, and I know I'm beaming back at him. A lot of young people don't know themselves well enough to truly go for what they want, in my experience. And half of them these days seem to just want to get famous on TikTok. To hear Laurie speak about his rather humble dream is endearing and inspiring.

"That sounds wonderful," I tell him genuinely.

But he shrugs and laughs. "Yeah, but I'm not going to be able to do anything like that unless I move to downtown Chicago, but I don't know how I can afford to move if I haven't got a job lined up. It's a catch twenty-two."

I hum. He's not wrong. What he needs is a bit of help.

I have to stop myself from opening my big mouth and offering him that help. We barely know each other. He doesn't want a handout from a stranger.

But what if we weren't strangers? What if what we have right now is just starting to blossom and grow? Could I offer him that opportunity he needs? It would only take a place to stay and the right door to open for him to get his chance.

This is dangerous. More to the point, it's really not *me.* I was always the sensible one with the long-term plans. I weigh every option before making any decisions. Shawn was the free spirit who I had to save on multiple occasions from leaping before he looked. My best friend had to bully me into coming here, and even then, I only did so to dip my toe back in the water.

Not to dive in headfirst.

But Laurie makes it so easy. He's like the sun, bright and full of life-giving energy. I can't help but be drawn into his orbit.

And quite frankly, with all the heart-shattering sadness I've endured, why should I shy away from the first spark of true happiness that's come my way? Like any relationship, nobody knows where this is going to lead. But I'm surprisingly ready to jump in with both feet.

However, I'm not going to scare the poor boy. He's had enough people in his life trying to manipulate him. Obviously, that's not what I'm trying to do, but I want him to come to his own conclusions naturally. If he's as into this relationship as much as I think I am, then I'll welcome him with open arms. More than that.

An open heart.

"Well, you never know what the future holds," is what I say to him. "Just make sure you're open to the possibility of new opportunities, and don't be afraid to take a leap of faith. Tomorrow could be a whole new day."

He smiles at me and rubs my knee. "I know" is all he says.

My heart contracts. He's right. I had no possible clue that when I agreed to come to this weekend retreat that he'd be waiting for me. That my life might change once again on a dime, as Shawn used to say. We met at a karaoke bar because I was supposed to go on a fancy date that canceled on me at the last minute. He was there because his roommate was having a noisy, unexpected breakup that he wanted to stay out of the way for. Our paths never should have crossed, and yet they did.

If fate is knocking on my door again, I'd be a fool to ignore it. Especially with the way Laurie is looking at me in this moment. The power might be out thanks to this storm, but we've got plenty of electricity between us right here.

I appreciate he's worried about his job. But I can't deny that if we get stuck here for a day or two, it could go a long way to convincing the both of us that this is worth taking that jump off the cliff for.

CHAPTER 14

Laurie

GETTING BACK TO THE CHALET FEELS MORE LIKE A BATTLE than a walk. The storm is blowing just as hard, and snow is still falling. We picked up breakfast supplies and more bottled water from the kitchen, so in theory we won't have to leave again for the next twelve to eighteen hours.

We just have to get there first.

The lights are glowing dimly as they're working off the emergency generator. But I can still see that another couple of inches of snow have fallen, and there are several trees around the property that are looking bent or broken or that have simply fallen over entirely. Luckily, it doesn't appear that any of the buildings have sustained serious damage, but I guess we won't be able to tell until day breaks and the storm stops. It has to stop eventually, right?

Beckett keeps a tight hold of my hand as we fight our way back to his lodgings. I would have struggled to even remember the way, I'm so disorientated, but he doesn't pause in our slog. Eventually, we're rewarded by the sight of the four similarly designed chalets that are clumped together in this particular part of the venue. His is the second one along, and I can feel him speeding us up in an attempt to get us out of the elements.

Once the door is unlocked, we tumble inside as fast as we can so as not to let too much snow inside. I gasp and pant, my face stinging as Beckett firmly locks it again. He doesn't stop there, though. After he's shaken himself off and gotten out of his boots, he goes to the closet and finds a spare towel. He rolls it up and jams it against the bottom of the door to stop as much of a draft coming through as possible.

"Good idea," I say through chattering teeth.

"Oh, baby bear," he says in concern, rubbing my shoulders. "Let's get you out of those wet things."

I love that he doesn't ask but just starts taking off my outer layers. I know that consent is very important, but when it worked with George (and the reason I stuck around when I knew he was no good) were those magic moments when he knew what I needed based on our previous agreements and just did it. I've only had a small glimpse of it, but in my experience, that's when Dom/sub relationships work the absolute best. It's what I crave. I don't want or expect him to make every little decision or do everything for me. But as he gently takes my coat off, I feel like this is perfect.

He helps me kick off my jeans and hangs them on the back of one of his dining chairs to dry. I still have my boxers and socks on, but I feel a bit like Winnie the Pooh as he leads me back into the bedroom. We've only got the one lamp on in here and another in the living room area to conserve energy, so it feels dark but cozy.

He doesn't hesitate as he goes to my suitcase again and pulls out the sweatpants I packed in case there was a dance class or something else physical. He beckons me over and gets me to step in them so he can pull them up.

"There we go," he says proudly before kissing my cheek. "Much better. Now, into bed with you."

"What about you?" I ask as he draws the covers back.

"Don't you worry about that," he tells me with a wink. I slip fully clothed onto the mattress then he pulls the duvet up to my chin. "I'll be back in a jiffy. You just think warm thoughts."

He bends down and gives my mouth a sweet little kiss. Then he grabs some things from the chest of drawers before disappearing back into the main room of the chalet.

I concentrate on breathing in and out, and soon enough the ice starts to thaw from my bones. I blow on my hands for a while, then shove them in between the two pillows under my head and curl my knees up to my chest to form a ball. I feel like a little woodland creature hibernating during winter. Before long, the shaking stops, and my heartbeat begins to slow again.

Just as I'm starting to feel the tiniest bit sleepy, I sense movement and look over my shoulder. Beckett is standing at the threshold of the room illuminated by the couple of lamps. He's wearing sweatpants and a hoodie, like me, and is holding two steaming mugs. He gives me that lopsided grin that first captured my heart.

"Sorry, I don't mean to go all stalkerish on you. That was a little creepy. But you just looked so comfy and peaceful that I had to take a moment to appreciate it."

I laugh. "You're not creepy. That's sweet. I *am* comfortable. But you need to warm up, too. Are you getting under the covers?"

He presses his lips together and looks at me a little longer with such warmth. Then he lets out a happy huff and comes back to life, walking into the room to my side of the bed. I turn so I can sit, and I see that he's made us hot chocolate with whipped cream and little marshmallows.

"Is this all right?" he asks, proving that he's got his finger on the pulse of when to take charge and when to check in with me.

"It's wonderful," I assure him. "There's a big difference between being told what I can and can't eat and my Daddy spoiling me with cocoa in bed."

He gives a sigh of relief and hands me the mug. "It might take me a bit of time to feel confident in making those distinctions. I hope you won't mind me touching base every now and again."

"Of course not," I say earnestly. Mostly because it's true, but also because that implies we're going to be spending enough time together that he's going to be able to get the hang of it.

That warms me up even better than the blankets and hot drink.

He slips under the covers beside me, lifting his arm up so I can snuggle against him. We're quiet as we sip our drinks, but it's not uncomfortable. It's peaceful, in fact. I look out of the window and feel like the snow might actually be starting to calm down. It looks like it's drifting down in the darkness rather than swirling in a mad fit. Thank goodness. As much as I'm loving spending this time with Beckett, I don't like feeling trapped and out of control. If the storm is letting up, I won't worry so much about what's going to happen over the next couple of days.

When I'm done with my chocolate, Beckett reaches over and touches my mug. I look up and see him raise his eyebrows, asking if he can take it from me. I nod, already feeling like there's something charging between us, and my heart rate starts to pick up again.

He encourages me to slip down, reangling the pillows under our heads and keeping the duvet on top. If I'm honest, I'm pretty hot right now, but it feels so cozy I don't want to change anything.

Beckett nuzzles his nose against mine, his breath warm and sweet from the hot chocolate as it ghosts over my lips. "Baby bear," he murmurs.

"Daddy," I whisper back.

Then he's kissing me, claiming me with his mouth and hands. He hugs me tightly to him, our bodies locked together. Normally, I'd say the fewer clothes the better. But there's something special about having been so cold and being stranded in the snow as we make out fully clothed under the covers. It's like being in a blanket fort. I feel so safe and cherished.

"Can I touch you, sweetheart?" he asks, squeezing my butt and making me shiver.

"You can touch me anywhere, Daddy," I promise him. "I have supplies if you need them."

He snorts with laugher, and I grin. There's a time and place for serious sex, but I like it when things are fun as well. As well as that, his laughter feels like a gift every single time after hearing all he's been through before I met him.

"Oh, someone's eager, I see," he quips.

"Very eager," I tell him, kissing his neck and nipping at his earlobe. "I want you inside me, if you'd like that."

He groans. *"Like* that? Baby boy, I'd *love* that. And it just so happens I also came prepared."

He reaches over to his nightstand and opens the drawer to reveal condoms and lube. It's my turn to laugh. "This is you not rushing into anything?" I tease. "I thought you came to this weekend just to dip your toe in the water?"

When he turns back around, his expression is smoldering. "I did, baby bear. But then I met you, so I went to the front desk and made sure I was properly prepared in case anything occurred between us—which, I might add, I very much hoped it would."

My mouth has gone dry. "You got those just for me?" I

manage to utter.

He kisses me, then nods. "I wanted to take care of you, sweet boy."

Wow. I mean…really, wow.

"Thank you, Daddy" is all I'm able to whisper before I'm kissing him again, my emotions running wild. He is so incredible, I can't even. He makes me feel like the center of the universe.

We keep kissing as he gently eases my sweatpants and boxers down my thighs. "This might be a bit cold," he warns before slipping his lubed-up fingers between my cheeks. I moan, but to be honest, we're so hot and sweaty under the covers, the wet coolness is actually kind of nice. He rubs my hole for a bit, making me shiver, then begins to ease his middle finger through my tight ring of muscle.

I bury my face against his neck and thrust back against his digit, welcoming the intrusion. He takes his time, but eventually, he adds a second finger and properly starts to stretch me out. There's no rush aside from my rising desire. We have all the time in the world.

"Good boy," he keeps murmuring, and honestly I'm not sure my heart can honestly take it. I'm soaring so high already and we haven't even started really making love yet.

"Daddy," I whimper as he adds a third finger. I've never had anyone spend so long on prep before. I feel like a writhing mess, but he's holding me tight, and the covers feel heavy on me, like I'm anchored.

"Shh, it's okay. Daddy's got you. Just relax. You're doing so well for me, baby bear."

We kiss as he fingers me deeper and harder. He strokes my prostate, and I wail into his mouth, wanting to chase my climax, but I know it's going to be so much better once it's his cock inside me.

He doesn't tease me for too long because he's a kind

Daddy. Wordlessly, he turns me around so my back is pressed against his chest. I feel movement behind me, then he's got his arm wrapped around my chest, and the slippery, blunt head of his cock is pressing against my entrance.

"Yesss," I hiss, clinging to him, pushing back, and inviting him in. "Please, Daddy, please."

"Good boy. Daddy's got you," he says in between kissing my neck. There's a slight burn, but mostly, I just feel the best kind of full. He's forcing his way inside me, binding us together, and I'm desperate for everything he's got to give. I'm panting and trembling, loving how claimed I feel.

It doesn't take long for him to bottom out. For a while, we just kiss, with me turning my head so he can find my mouth over my shoulder. I love having him deep inside me, his tip nudging at my sensitive bundle of nerves. But then he starts to rock, and I'm wailing again as he hits my prostate over and over again, lighting my whole body on fire.

It's like being in a furnace with all the clothes and covers, but I love it, like we're melting together. He starts slow, thrusting inside me as his hand travels under my sweater and T-shirt. He rubs my belly and squeezes one of my pecs, flicking his thumb over my nipple and making it hard. The sensations threaten to overwhelm me, but I cling to the moment, desperate not to miss a single thing.

After a while he tries to speed up, but our position isn't helping too much. "Lie on your tummy, baby bear," he tells me. We manage to roll without him having to pull out, then he's on top of me, his weight solid and delicious.

He starts pistoning his hips, slamming into me hard and fast, and we're both grunting and pouring with sweat. The room stinks of masculine musk, and the air is filled with our frantic cries. I grind against the mattress, needing more friction, and of course my Daddy realizes that.

"Can you lift your hips and get on your knees?" he asks.

I nod, keeping my head on my arms but shuffling to push my ass higher. He slows just a little, but then he's got his hand back around me with a wadded-up tissue pressed against the tip of my sensitive cock.

"Touch yourself, gorgeous," he tells me as he starts fucking me hard again. "Make yourself come for Daddy. Such a good, *good* boy."

I whimper with pleasure as I do as I'm told, my climax rushing up to greet me. I barely manage to give a yell of warning before I'm coming into the tissue that's protecting our bedsheets. I feel Beckett snap his hips behind me and his cock start to throb as he spills his load against the condom that's deep inside me.

We collapse in a heap, and he rolls us side by side again, like how we started. We gasp for air as we gradually come down from our orgasms, but he stays inside me until he's soft, hugging me tightly. It doesn't take a genius to work out that this must be the first sex he's had since he lost Shawn. When my senses come back to me, I pick up his hand from where it's pressed against my chest and kiss the wedding band. I want to tell him however he's feeling, it's okay.

He nuzzles at my cheek until I turn and kiss his mouth passionately. "Thank you, baby bear," he whispers.

"Thank you, Daddy," I say, equally raw but happy.

I know being snowed in scares me, but in this moment, I give thanks to a universe that is far smarter than both me and Beckett. If that car accident hadn't brought us back together, I might have missed out on one of the best moments of my life.

Because I know it's not even early days—it's still technically the first full day. And I know full well that I'm high on sex endorphins right now.

But I can't help but shake the feeling that I might just be falling in love.

CHAPTER 15

Beckett

I DON'T REALLY WANT TO BURST THIS BLISSFUL BUBBLE THAT Laurie and I are living in. We've spent the morning wrapped up in blankets, cozily reading, working on crossword puzzles, and chatting. We're conscious of conserving energy, but we kept most of the lights off, and breakfast didn't involve much more than the coffee machine, as we were given little cereal boxes and fruit last night. Thankfully, the small fridge is still operational.

But I can sense that Laurie is getting anxious. He managed to text his mother when the storm finally passed, and cell signal got a little better again. He's holding off contacting work, I can tell. He's avoiding the confrontation, because I think he's still hoping there's a chance he can make it back and not get in trouble. I wish I could take that burden on for him. All I can do for now is support him and hopefully give him the courage to tell them there's nothing they can do. If they get upset, that's on them. Laurie can't change the weather.

It is midday now, though, and I think it's about time we

went to investigate the situation. It wouldn't hurt to get some hot food for lunch if possible as well.

We take separate showers and get dressed to go outside. I don't pick his outfit out today, as I don't want to smother him, but I do put his hat on his head, which makes him beam. Before we brave it outside, I have to stop and kiss him for a minute. He's just so…*wonderful.*

"Ready?" I ask.

"Ready," he says confidently.

There's a small arched awning over the door, so the snow doesn't stop us from opening the door. I blink against the brilliant sunshine as we step out into the cold, fresh air. I shield my eyes from the sun and marvel at how still everything feels compared to last night. There's a good couple of feet of snow on the ground and plenty still in the trees, but the howling wind has completely vanished, and cheerful birdsong fills the air as if celebrating that we made it through.

"Prepared to fight our way to the path?" I ask as I close and lock the door. Laurie nods enthusiastically.

"It doesn't seem so scary now the storm has stopped," he says, plowing ahead into the thick snow. I get what he means. It can only get better from here, presumably.

I found small trash liners under the sink, so we might look a bit silly, but we've bagged our feet up to protect us from the worst of the snow until we reach the lodge again. In the absence of Wellington boots, I have to say they work pretty well, and we're not soaked and freezing by the time we get to our destination. We take them off to go inside so we don't traipse snow everywhere, balling them up and throwing them away.

The dining hall is busy, and it looks like they've got another buffet going to keep things easy and casual. But I'm drawn to Shellridge's bear cub who seems to be directing people near the front door.

"You'll find everything you need out there," he's saying as Laurie and I approach. "We're taking it in turns with the shovels."

I raise my eyebrows at him as we get his attention. "Everything all right?" I ask.

Billy grins at me. "We're digging our way out! The plows are on the main roads, but we're clearing the lot right now. We have sand and salt as well as shovels and spades, and some people are even using hockey sticks and tennis rackets we found out back! Do you want to volunteer?"

"Absolutely!" Laurie cries enthusiastically, making my heart ache. Then he glances at me. "I mean, I do if you do?"

I chuckle. "I think that's a marvelous idea." I look at Billy. "Are you all right if we have some lunch first?"

He nods. "Actually, I insist. You'll need your energy. But we appreciate every pair of hands we can get!"

I nod at him and wink at Laurie. "Full tummies first, then. I think I might even have a shovel in the back of my car if we're lucky."

"Amazing," Billy says excitedly. "See you in a bit!"

We get ourselves platefuls of a Tex-Mex themed lunch of lots of rice, beans, veggies, barbecue wings, and big glasses of fizzy drinks. Laurie chats happily about other times he's volunteered, mostly through his school. It seems he's done litter clean up, handed out water at charity races, dished up food at a homeless shelter, and often visits other residents at the care home where his grandma lives to spend a little time with them playing checkers or just talking.

I feel ashamed. "I've never done anything like that," I say, shaking my head as I finish the last of my lunch.

He tilts his head and frowns. "Yeah, but you work for an actual charity," he says with a chuckle.

I shrug. "That's not the same as giving up my time for free just because it helps other people. You've inspired me."

He looks shy and hesitates before he speaks. "Maybe we could do something together sometime, then?" he eventually suggests, blushing again.

My heart swells. I offer him my hand, which he immediately takes, and I give him a squeeze. "I'd really love that," I say sincerely.

When we make our way out to the front of the lodge, there's a team of at least a dozen people being led by Daddy Bear who is coordinating with a guy driving a pickup truck that has a snow blade on the front. The steps are already clear, and there are several pathways and lots of cars dug out. The lodge owner waves at us as we trot down into the lot.

"Come to help?"

"That we have," I call back cheerfully. "I think I've got a shovel in my car."

He gives me a thumbs-up, then diverts his attention back to the other volunteers while Laurie and I go to my Jeep to investigate. Luckily, the path has mostly been cleared that way, as we didn't bring another set of the trash liners. To my relief, I *do* have a shovel stashed in my trunk under all the other bits and bobs I have in case of emergency.

"I think I left it there the last time I had to dig myself out of my driveway," I marvel.

"You're so prepared," Laurie says, shaking his head and sounding slightly awestruck. He doesn't know that I'm already mentally working on a list of things to get for his car when it's fixed up again.

"A lot of it's experience," I assure him as we head back to where the main group is working to find out where Daddy Bear wants to put us. "After you get caught out once without an ice scraper or something, you make sure you have one for next time. Easy."

He scoffs like it's not so easy, but that's what he's not getting.

It's easy for me, and now *he* has me, too.

Just before we reach the work party, my phone rings. I pause and frown as I get it out of my pocket, but then I laugh. "It's my best friend, Heather," I tell Laurie. "She's probably checking up on me. I haven't been responding to her texts. Do you mind if I get this?"

"Sure," he says cheerfully, taking the shovel from me. "I'll be out here when you're done."

I nod at him, then answer the call before it goes to voice-mail. "Hi!" I say.

"Oh, so you *are* alive," Heather replies, only sounding slightly grumpy.

"Sorry," I say bashfully. "I know I should have replied to your messages."

"Are you okay?" she says, skipping over my half-arsed apology. "The snow is bad here, but you're out in the sticks."

"We're okay," I say honestly, continuing to wander back inside the lodge. If I'm just standing around instead of work-ing, I'd rather be warm for a little longer. "The storm was pretty bad, but it's over now. You're lucky I've got enough signal to get through, though. I was just about to start helping a group who are clearing out the parking lot so people can get to the main road."

"Aww," she says. "You're hanging out with people and not just hiding in your room! Have you made any friends?" I pause a little too long for her liking, apparently. "What? What's wrong? Oh no, was it awful? Did I push you when you weren't ready? Beck, I'm so sorry—"

"Whoa, whoa," I cry, cutting her off. "You're fine. Great, actually. This was the right first step."

"It was?" she asks curiously.

I look around the lobby. Nobody's paying attention to

me, obviously. They all have their own business to be worrying about. But this feels private, and I sort of wish I was back in my chalet.

But why? I can tell there's a tiny part of me that feels disloyal. Like, if I admit my feelings out loud it's a kind of betrayal to Shawn. He wouldn't want that, though. If he was here, I'm sure he'd be shouting his happiness from the rooftops.

I look down at my wedding ring and run my thumb along it.

"I've met someone, Heather."

She gasps. I can feel her vibrating through the phone, but her voice is measured when she finally speaks. "You have?" Her words are full of warmth.

I nod, even though she can't see me. "His name is Laurie," I say softly. "He's...oh, he's just lovely. We've spent almost the whole time together."

Now, she squeals. *"Ohmygodohmygodohmygod!* Really? You're serious? You've had some fun?"

I bite my lip, deciding to be honest and get a second opinion that isn't the imaginary one from Shawn. "We have had fun, definitely. But that's not it. I don't think this is just a weekend fling."

"Fuck me," Heather says before spluttering. "I mean, wow —seriously? You didn't even want to go!"

"Do you think it's too fast?" I ask. "I can't seem to make myself be level-headed about this."

She blows a raspberry. "Love doesn't work on a preorganized schedule, babe. I mean! Not love, that's too fast! Any feelings. But—"

"No," I interrupt softly, a smile spreading over my face and butterflies fluttering in my belly. "I think this might be love, you know."

"Fuuuuck," she says quietly but in awe. "Dude, that's... wow. Can I be your maid of honor?"

I bark out a laugh. "Behave," I warn her, but I look down at my wedding ring once more. For the first time ever, I actually feel like that kind of path could be a possibility for me again.

"Beckett, honestly, I'm thrilled for you," she says in a rare serious tone, no teasing at all. "You deserve happiness. You deserve love."

"We're taking it slowly," I assure her. "He's been incredibly considerate." He almost got himself *killed* trying to be considerate, I think, but that's a story for when Heather and I are face-to-face with a bottle or two of really good wine. I don't want to dwell on it too much right now and start weeping and shaking in the bloody lobby. "He's kind and funny and ambitious and—"

"Hot?" she interrupts, making me snort.

"Very hot," I agree, feeling the wolfish grin on my face.

Last night was...well, that's something else I probably shouldn't be thinking about in a public space, although for entirely different reasons. Good lord, I can't wait to get my hands and mouth on every inch of his gorgeous body and make him utterly delirious with pleasure.

I open my mouth to give my best friend the PG-13 rated version of events, but the lights suddenly all go out. It might be daytime outside, but we're still plunged into a gloomy darkness. "Oh, shit," I utter as people start shouting among themselves.

Unlike last night, the power doesn't seem to be coming back on.

"Beck?" Heather questions from the other end of the line.

I swallow and look around. Nope. Still nothing.

"I'm going to have to call you back," I say slowly. "Love you."

"Love you too, babe," she says faintly, then I end the call. We're still without power. That can only mean one thing. The backup generator has gone down.

CHAPTER 16

Laurie

I'm really enjoying attacking the snow with Beckett's shovel. Daddy Bear has got me to work by myself on a path that leads to the last part of the parking lot that's slightly around the corner of the main building. There are only a few cars and trucks there, but we don't know who's going to be eager to try and leave this afternoon or who'll be okay to wait a little longer. The way I see it, every single load I shift goes toward the ultimate goal, so I'm happy to keep plugging away.

And I *am* happy. So happy. My mind wanders as I keep on with my physical task. Shovel after shovel doesn't require much concentration, so that means my thoughts are pretty much centered on one thing.

Beckett.

He wants to keep seeing each other after this. I'm almost certain that means he wants to be my Daddy. My first *real* Daddy. I've decided George doesn't count, as he never respected me. I was always his dirty little secret, and he was never, *ever* going to leave his poor wife for me.

The parallels between him and Beckett strike me in that

moment. Beckett could have hidden Shawn from me, or at least downplayed how complicated his feelings are for his husband, who was taken far too soon from him. I love that Shawn feels almost present between us, like he's giving his blessing. I don't feel threatened by him like I did George's wife, even though she never did anything wrong.

The difference—I think—is that Beckett has more than enough love in his heart for both Shawn and me. George was a greedy fucker who wanted to have his cake and eat it, too.

Perhaps I'm just being hopelessly optimistic and projecting what I hope is true. All I know is that I want to keep seeing Beckett once we dig our way out of this snow and the weekend finally comes to an end. He's said he wants that too, and I can't help but feel like this could be a real, long-term relationship.

One I won't have to hide or be ashamed of.

Movement up ahead catches my eye. I'm all alone in this part of the lot, and I'm suddenly uneasy. I'm not sure why, but instinct tells me to duck behind the nearest car before peeking out again to get another look. When I see who the person is, I understand why.

Mick.

I feel an irritated wave of frustration wash over me as I see him stomp his way through the snow toward his pickup truck. I'm the one who should be angry and hurt, not him. The way he treated me was appalling, and I only tried to help him by telling him the gas station was closed last night.

Then I shake myself, a wonderful calm overpowering the prickly anxiety that was telling me I'd done something wrong.

Who cares what he thinks of me? I only care what Beckett thinks.

Still, I watch on curiously as Mick throws back the tarp that was covering the back of his pickup, throwing off the snow that had gathered there. I realize he was carrying something in each of his hands as he approached. They look like brown watering cans with the nozzles cut short, or like the kind of thing my mom's weedkiller comes in. I frown as he puts them into the truck bed, then covers them again with the tarp.

Rather than heading back to the lodge's front entrance, he looks around warily, then starts marching off in the opposite direction. I think that might have been the way he came from, actually. He certainly didn't pass me to get to his truck, did he?

I don't know what comes over me. I should just leave him be to get himself into whatever trouble he feels like. But I can't seem to stop my feet from following as he makes his way around the back of the lodge into the woods.

I grip Beckett's shovel in my hands, my heart racing. What am I going to do if he turns around and demands to know what I'm doing? I suppose I can play dumb and say I was worried he needed help with something, but honestly, the more I watch him kicking and punching his way through the snow, the more I get the strong suspicion that he's up to something.

I keep to the trees as I follow behind him, squinting to make out what he's doing. I see a box-like structure and a wooden shed that he stops by. He opens the door to the shed and pulls out another of the brown canister things. By the way he's holding it, it seems light and empty, but the previous two looked heavy.

I rush to dart behind a particularly large oak that's conveniently nearby. I peek out to keep watching him, hoping he doesn't see me. Thankfully, he's too focused on whatever it is he's doing to be paying attention to anything else. He's opened the door of the white-and-black box thing that's almost as tall as he is, and he's crouched down. His body is covering what he's doing, unfortunately. But then a bird squawks, and his head snaps my way.

Immediately, I withdraw behind the oak, my heart pounding as I try not to breathe too hard. I don't dare look out again, but soon enough, I hear him thumping and cursing his way back to the parking lot. I think he didn't see me. *Phew.* When I do dare take a glimpse out, the door on the white box and the shed are closed once more.

What's going on?

I wait until it's quiet, then slip out from behind the tree to scurry back the way I just came, into the lot. I frown, trying to work out what Mick was doing with his truck as I creep closer. He's still got this can in his hand and he's doing something with his fuel cap…

Oh, shit. He's filling up his tank. With what?

I look back toward the small box structure he stopped by. Fuck! Was that the emergency generator? Some of them run off fuel, don't they? Has he *stolen* a can for his own car? Not just one, but three? He has, hasn't he?

"Hey!" I bellow before I can stop myself. I march forward, using the path he so conveniently bulldozed for me, holding the shovel in both hands. "What are you doing?"

He jerks around, sloshing some of the fuel onto the ground and his boots. "Fuck!" he snarls. Then he looks up at me and curls his lip. "None of your fucking business," he barks as I get closer.

"It is," I argue back. "You're stealing from the lodge! We need that generator to keep the power going for lights and heat. You haven't even just taken one can. You filled up three!"

He shrugs and goes back to pouring the thick, iridescent liquid down the gullet of his truck. "I look out for myself, kid. Somebody's got to."

"Yeah?" I say, absolutely fuming. "Well then, I'm looking

out for *everyone else.*" I angrily throw back the tarp and try to grab for the other two cans. But he sees what I'm doing and roars as he lunges for me, dropping the third can on the ground.

"You meddling little *shit!*" he yells as I dart away without either can, but I still have the shovel, which I hold up protectively as he advances, his body a hulking mass and his fists balled. "First, you lure me here only to humiliate me, then you give me blue balls, and then you do everything you can to stop me from leaving! What the fuck is *wrong* with you? Do you seriously believe you're *that* important?"

"You're putting everyone else here in danger," I cry, not believing I'm having to spell this out for him. I'm walking backward in the part that's already been cleared, trying to glance over my shoulder to make sure I don't slip or crash into anything. "You're putting *yourself* in danger. Just wait until the roads are properly salted and plowed!"

"There you go again!" he scoffs. "I'm not a pathetic little child who needs to be told what to do every second of the day. That's *you.* Honestly, boys like you should just shut up and be grateful anyone wants to fuck you at all. It's all you're good for. Such a sniveling little prick, running off with that British wanker. I bet you two planned this from the start to make a fool of me!"

"What?" I say incredulously. "Now who's deluded? I'm just lucky he was there to rescue me from you—"

I'm too busy yelling at him to watch where I'm going. My feet go out from under me on some ice, and the next thing I know, I'm flat on my ass and the shovel goes flying from my hands. I gasp in shock, pain bursting up my back and coldness seeping immediately into my clothes.

"You didn't need 'rescuing,' you overdramatic little crybaby," he snarls, looming over me and blocking out the sun. I try and scramble backward, but he leans down and grabs me by the scruff of my clothes. "You led me on, then pussied out. You just want attention. Well, guess what, you little cock tease? You've got my attention now. And I'm going to make sure you don't tell a fucking soul what you saw here. That's my gas now. I'm getting out of this fucking place and going home, and they're going to pay for my trouble. That's the least they could do."

He bares his teeth, yanking my face close to his. I can smell the beer on his breath, and I gag. Oh, he's planning on *drunk* driving? This just keeps getting better and better!

I shove at his chest and try and kick at his knees. "Get OFF me!" I cry.

"What's the matter?" He laughs cruelly, still gripping tightly to my coat. "I thought you liked attention. You certainly seemed to love that British douchebag being all over you. The way I see it, you *owe* me, Lil Star Bear. Why don't you suck my cock here and now, and I'll forget about all the other shit you put me through?"

"*NO!*" I scream, genuinely terrified. Oh, fuck. What's he going to do? What's he going to *make* me do? No, no, never. I have to fight. I'm worth so much more than he thinks I am. "Fuck you! You're a psycho! I don't owe you anything!"

I still have my gloves on, so I can't scratch his face. Instead, I take both my thumbs and jam them against his eyes. He bellows and almost lets go, but then he's shaking me hard.

"I would have left you alone," he snarls, "but you had to come poking around. I just wanted to leave!"

"By stealing power from everyone else!" I yell back because apparently when I'm in very real danger, I can't stop my big mouth from arguing back. But I'm done. I'm *done* with being messed with and bullied by the likes of him and George. He doesn't get to rewrite history and make himself the victim. He's in the wrong here, and I'm not letting him get away with it.

However, he's still got me pinned down in the snow and the ice with a manic look in his eyes. "Fuck everyone else and fuck you," he growls. "I look after number one. I never should have come here, but now that I have—"

I don't get to find out what he wants before he leaves. I can take a chilling guess. But thankfully, I'm spared knowing because one second he's there, then the next he's flying off me and back into the snow.

I gasp and twist around on the ground to see Beckett standing there, looking absolutely livid, the shovel in his hands and a furious glare in his eyes.

"Stay the HELL away from my boy!" he shouts.

I've never been more relieved in my entire life.

CHAPTER 17

Beckett

"YOU BROKE MY NOSE!" MICK WAILS FROM BEHIND A BLOOD-smeared hand. He's landed in a pile of snow and isn't getting up for a minute, so I ignore him. Instead, I turn all my attention to my darling baby bear, rushing to his side to help him get to his feet.

"Are you all right?" I cry as I settle him on the ground, my stomach still churning from what I almost just witnessed.

He gasps and throws his arms around me. "Oh, Beckett." He sobs against my neck.

"It's okay. I'm here. Daddy's here," I reassure him, kissing his temple and rubbing his back. But then Mick moves, and I raise the shovel I've still got in my other hand. Laurie springs back to face his attacker as well. "Stay the fuck down," I warn Mick.

Of course he ignores me, fumbling to his feet and wiping more blood from his face where I smashed him with the shovel. "Fuck off, dickhead," he gripes. "The two of you are always poking your nose in other people's business."

I scoff, rage boiling inside me. "You're looking at assault charges, *mate.* If that's poking my nose where it doesn't belong, I'm more than happy to do it anytime. I told you to keep your dirty hands away from my boy, and this time, you're going to listen."

"What's going on here?" a deep voice rumbles, and I glance over in relief to see not only Daddy Bear coming over but his cub, Billy, and several other guests as well.

"Nothing," Mick yells back before spitting blood into the snow. "Although if anyone's going to be pressing charges, it'll be me. I'll be billing you for any hospital bills as well, jackass. You've definitely broken my nose."

"And I'd do it again," I snarl, then turn my attention to the lodge owner. "I was looking for Laurie when I heard shouting. I saw this man pinning my boyfriend to the ground. Laurie was clearly in distress and trying to get away, so I did what I had to in order to set him free."

Daddy Bear arches an eyebrow at Mick, then looks at Laurie. But Laurie is gawking open-mouthed at me. "Your boyfriend?" he whispers.

I can't help but chuckle, even though this really isn't the time for it. "Yes, sweetheart," I say.

"Awww," Billy coos, clutching his hands to his chest.

Daddy Bear's mouth twitches, but then he's all serious again. "Is this true?" he asks Laurie, who also stops smiling. He shivers against me as he looks back at Mick, who's scowling at him.

"He was on top of me, yeah," he says in a small voice. "He was yelling and saying all kinds of horrible things. He said... he said he was going to make me suck his cock."

A red mist descends over me, and I'm lunging for the bastard before I realize Daddy Bear has grabbed my coat and is hauling me back. "I'll *kill* you," I roar.

"I never said anything like that," Mick retaliates with a horrible laugh. I calm down enough that Daddy Bear releases me, and Laurie wraps his arms around me again. I can feel him trembling, and his eyes are glassy. I have no doubt as to who I believe.

"Leave," Daddy Bear growls with a jut of his chin. "Unless you want to press charges, little one?"

Laurie blinks, thinking, then he gasps and shakes his head. "No, you can't let him leave! He stole three canisters worth of fuel from the generator! You can get at least two of them back from the back of his truck!"

"Liar!" Mick shouts, his eyes wild. "That's my property! You have no right to put your hands on it, none of you! I remembered I had spare fuel and didn't need to go to the gas station after all. I was busy loading up when this little shit tried to steal it from me! It's my word against his. You can't prove nothing!"

"Oh, yeah?" Billy says with a raised eyebrow. While Mick was busy yelling, it looks like he snuck around the backs of the cars and has picked up an open can from the ground. The smell of diesel wafts over to us so strong it makes me cough.

"That's mine," Mick insists in a surly tone.

"You have the exact same make of canisters that we happen to use here at Shellridge?" the bear cub asks with a raised eyebrow.

"And you happen to have spare fuel just when the generator failed?" I chime in.

Laurie gasps and looks up at me. "It did?"

I nod. "The lodge has no power at all."

I expect Laurie to look upset or afraid. He's been so worried about being stranded in the snow this whole time. But instead, he looks furious.

"I *told* you!" he snaps at Mick with such anger that Mick has the good grace to look sheepish and take a step back. "I told you that you'd be endangering everyone else. But you only cared about yourself. You realize that even if you did leave, it would be because all these people dug out the parking lot! You're so selfish. I can't believe I ever gave you the time of day."

"Tell you what," Daddy Bear says, crossing his massive arms and fixing Mick with a glare. "We take back those two full cans no questions asked—"

"And what's left in this one!" the bear cub adds, sloshing around a fair amount in the can he's holding.

"And what's left in that one," Daddy Bear agrees. "Then we'll let you leave, no questions asked. And you never come back here again."

Mick scoffs, cocky once more. "That's easy. This place is a shithole, and you're all a bunch of fucking pussies."

I really think he could have gotten away with just that if he hadn't opened his big mouth. But the flash of anger that crosses Daddy Bear's face makes it clear that he's just made it real personal.

"Oh, I'll be contacting the folks at the Bears-4-U headquarters as well," Daddy Bear says casually. "Informing them you'll need a lifelong ban. They can track IP addresses, you know. They have ways of stopping you from setting up new profiles."

Mick splutters, looking genuinely horrified for the first time during this entire unpleasant encounter. "You can't do that!" he cries.

"I guess you'll have to rely on your sparkling personality to meet boys now," I gloat with perhaps a little too much glee, but I can't help it. It's so rare that bad people receive what they deserve in this world.

"This is all your fault," he bites out, jabbing a finger at me. "You ruined everything."

"Actually, you brought every single thing that's happened here on your own head," Laurie says loudly and confidently. "And unless you do want me to call the police and get you charged with assault, I suggest you get the hell out of here as soon as possible."

Mick opens and closes his mouth before wasting no time turning on his heels and stalking back to his truck. Billy waves cheerfully at him as he passes.

"You can still report him," I tell Laurie. I don't want him to regret not pressing charges.

But Laurie shakes his head. "In the end, he just threatened me and pushed me down. I don't want to hash it over and over. I want to forget about him." He wraps his arms around my back and looks at me with such affection it catches my breath. "I just want to spend my last evening with you."

I think I hear Billy let out another "Aww!" but I'm so busy looking at Laurie, I can't be sure.

"It's not our last evening, sweetheart," I say, shaking my head.

"No?" Laurie says, hope in his voice.

"No," I say. I know we've danced around this, but I've lost too much in this life. I'm not afraid to make it official when my heart knows what it wants. "This is just the beginning. You're my boyfriend now, remember?"

He gives me a watery smile. "Can I just be your boy, Daddy?" he whispers.

I lean down and capture his mouth. "Of course you can, baby bear," I murmur.

I wasn't sure I could ever find happiness again. It's frightening to think that I didn't want to come to this retreat. That I was so determined to close off my heart for good that I almost missed being blessed with a second moment of serendipity.

I hug him tightly to me and glance up at the blue skies valiantly peeking through the clouds. I wonder if Shawn brought me to this place and time. Him, and Heather's proverbial foot up my arse, of course. Either way, I feel incredibly blessed, and I know that no matter what happens, I'm not letting go of Laurie for anything.

"Come on," I say as Mick angrily reverses his truck out of the space and begins to make his exit. We don't need to watch that. "Let's go shovel some snow, and then Daddy can warm you up again."

"Promise?" Laurie asks, desire and excitement dancing in his eyes.

"Promise," I assure him.

After that horrible fright, my baby bear deserves some pampering. And some fun, just like my best friend said.

We both do.

CHAPTER 18

Laurie

BY THE TIME THE SUN STARTS TO SET, THE PARKING LOT IS mostly dug out, and half the cars have gone. The dining hall in the lodge is a lot quieter, and table service has resumed. We even got word that after all the fuss Mick made, the gas station is open once again. The disaster has passed, and life is returning to normal.

Well, that's not exactly true. I don't think my life will ever be normal again. But the danger appears to have gone, at least.

I'm glad that Beckett and I stopped to have dinner as soon as we came in from the snow, even if we were a little damp and uncomfortable. The roads are apparently good enough that he should be able to drive me home tomorrow, so this is going to be our last night together, and I want to spend it just the two of us.

Now that we're heading back to his chalet, the energy between us is electric, and I have a feeling that despite my muscles being sore and my body being tired, I'm not going to be sleeping anytime soon. In fact, I'd put money on Beckett giving me *another* workout. The best kind.

He's kissing me before the door is even properly closed. He fumbles with the latch as he devours my mouth, while I attack his coat. It might still be freezing outside, but it's toasty warm in here and I need him in a lot fewer clothes right now.

Our beautiful lovemaking last night is a moment that I'll never forget. But it's been over two days now, and aside from quick glimpses I haven't actually seen him properly naked, which is something I need to fix as soon as humanly possible.

Lucky for me, he seems to feel the same way. He's tearing off all my outer layers, not pausing as he frantically kisses my mouth. We've kicked off our snowy shoes, and I'm down to just my jeans and a T-shirt, but then he finally does stop, panting and cupping either side of my face.

"I want to do something special for you, baby bear," he says. "But I'll need a few minutes. Can I tempt you to stay on the sofa for a little while if I made you some more hot chocolate?"

I giggle. "I'd do anything for you, Daddy. But definitely if you make me hot chocolate."

He kisses me gently, then hugs me tightly. "I know this is just the beginning, but I want to commemorate the end of this absolutely incredible—if slightly strange—weekend."

I nod. "I know what you mean."

He steers me to the sofa, and I snuggle down. After all, working that snow shovel for the past few hours has woken up several muscles I wasn't previously aware of. I hum contentedly as he kisses the tip of my nose.

He goes and fusses with the coffee machine that will give us the hot water for cocoa, then dashes into the bathroom. I'd been expecting to hurry to the bed to have sex, but I hear the tub start to fill and guess that my Daddy has something more elaborate planned.

I close my eyes and relax until I feel him touch my shoulder. I blink my eyes back open to see him place the hot chocolate on the table in front of me. "There you go, sweetheart."

"Thank you, Daddy."

After all the hard work and especially the adrenaline spike earlier, the yummy sugar is much appreciated. He's put whipped cream and marshmallows on top again as well, and I can't help but yearn to get used to this level of pampering.

I drink it down, buzzing with happiness, and then snuggle back on the sofa again to close my eyes. I don't want Beckett to rush with what he's doing. I'm perfectly content where I am, and for once, I don't feel anxious about the future.

He makes me feel like everything's going to be okay. More than that, he makes me feel like I don't have to have everything figured out *right* now. I feel like since I graduated high school that I've been sort of flailing and aimless. But this is what makes Beckett a proper Daddy. Without even saying too much directly about it, he's helped me feel much more at peace with my life.

In a crappy job right now? No worries, there's still plenty of time for me to discover what truly makes my heart sing. Still living at home? In this economy—that makes total sense. Only dated losers? That's fine, we've already fixed that one, haven't we?

For the first time ever, I'm honestly excited for what tomorrow might bring. Because he's promised to be by my side, and I trust that he'll look out for me.

"I am a good person," I say softly to myself with a big, genuine smile. "And I am worthy of love."

It's amazing how much a life can change in just a few days. Getting to know Beckett has made me appreciate how that can be for the worst. But in this moment, I hope that for the both of us it's for the best. I know I can't believe that it was barely forty-eight hours since we met. And now here we are.

About to start on the next chapters of our lives, together.

I must have dozed off because the next thing I realize is he's gently squeezing my shoulder again and brushing the backs of his knuckles against my cheek. "Sweet boy?" he says. He's stripped down to just a shirt and pants. The shirt sleeves are rolled up, showing his tattoos, and I wake up quite quickly at such a delicious sight.

"Daddy?"

He smiles. "I ran you a hot bath. But if you just want to sleep, I can take you to bed."

I shake my head and sit up, even if I am a little disoriented. "No, no, I'm awake," I insist, making him chuckle.

"Is that right, baby bear?"

I rub my eyes, then grin at him. "Yes, Daddy."

"Come on, then. Daddy has a surprise for you."

He takes my hand and helps me stand up from the couch. Then I gasp, appreciating that I must have been quite heavily asleep not to have noticed any of this.

There are rose petals scattered in a path from the bedroom to the big bathroom that I haven't really used yet, as the en suite off Beckett's bedroom was so convenient. The main bathroom has the tub, though. I look between the two rooms and see that they're covered in red, white, and pink petals as well as dozens of tea lights. The hot water in the bath is visibly steaming, and it smells of some amazing scented oil. More petals are floating on the surface.

"You packed all this?" I ask incredulously.

Beckett chuckles. "No. I had a little help from a certain bear cub who is apparently very invested in our happy ever after. He snuck up to me while we were working outside and informed me that he'd let himself in here and left a care package for us." He snorts and rolls his eyes. "There were also a *lot* of condoms and different flavors of lube."

I drop my head back and laugh. "I like his style."

Beckett hums and pulls me against him, nuzzling his nose against mine. My heart rate doubles in a matter of seconds. "He certainly gave me plenty of ideas," Beckett says, his voice a low rumble.

He walks me backward along the rose-petal path, still kissing my smiling mouth as we head into the bathroom. It's hot and steamy in here and absolutely perfect after a day spent out in the snow. He pulls my T-shirt off and runs his hands up and down my sides with a primal sort of growl.

"Gorgeous," he rumbles, nipping at my earlobe and making me shiver. "My gorgeous boy."

Lust pulses through me as I paw at his shirt buttons, but he bats my hands away with a grin.

"No, sweetheart. Don't you worry about a thing. Daddy's going to take care of it all."

"Okay," I say shyly. Fuck, he makes me feel like a prince.

He drops to his knees and unbuttons my jeans, lowering the zipper and then tugging them down my legs so I can kick them and my socks off. I'm just left in my boxers, but I'm not cold, and now he can see just how excited he's making me. He groans as he nuzzles his nose through the cotton against my already half-hard cock, squeezing my butt cheeks with both hands and massaging the globes.

"Baby bear," he mutters. I gasp and run my fingers through his hair, swaying on the spot where he's worshiping me.

Eventually, he does move and slip down my underwear, allowing my cock to spring free. He licks and sucks the leaking tip, making me whimper and tremble, but he doesn't tease me for too long.

"Into the hot water with you," he says as he stands. He

takes my hand to help steady me as I step into the half-full free-standing tub. I thought the water was a little low, but it's scalding hot in the best way, and I realize with two bodies in it, the water level will be perfect.

I get myself settled in the middle of the bath, then lean on the side and rest my chin on the back of my hands, watching my Daddy as he begins to unbutton his shirt. My heart flips over and my cock jumps in the hot water as desire washes through me. He doesn't break eye contact as he puts on a show, stripping slowly for me.

"Daddy," I whisper, just because I want to hear the word on my tongue.

"Good boy," he rasps back.

He really is stunning. His frame is a medium build, but he's also muscular and covered in dark hair. It swirls like storm clouds, and I want to lick and touch it all. His tattoos are extensive and colorful. I want to ask about the story behind each and every one of them from the dragon to the musical notes to the flock of doves.

But not right now. Right now, I have other priorities on my mind.

I scoot up as he steps into the bath behind me. The rose petals swirl around us, and the scented oil shimmers in the water. Now that we're both submerged, the level is just up to my chest, and my skin tingles with the heat. Not to mention from where I feel Beckett's body against mine. His chest to my back, his thighs supporting mine, his hard cock pressed along my crack.

Then there are his hands and his lips. Oh...*god*. He's kissing the side of my neck while his fingers trail along my tummy, playing with my budding nipples and squeezing my soft flesh.

"Mine," he growls as his right hand drifts lower, skimming down my thigh and making me tremble. "All mine."

I moan as he circles my cock with his fingers, rubbing his thumb against the slit and stroking the shaft.

"Daddy," I say, dropping my head back against his shoulder. He wastes no time in finding my mouth to kiss it, his hand moving faster against my cock.

"Is that nice?" he murmurs against my lips. I nod frantically, making a keening noise. "You can come whenever you want, sweetheart. Daddy wants to watch you."

I gasp as lust shoots through me like a bolt of lightning. That's not the kinkiest thing I've ever heard, but the idea of Beckett watching me as I come undone as its own pleasure makes me feel so naughty and delicious and wanton.

"I'm close," I warn him as he continues to play with me, the water churning around as he jerks me off. "Daddy, *oh!*"

I screw up my eyes as my climax starts to peak, desperate to come but also not wanting this magical moment to be over just yet.

But soon my orgasm overpowers me. I'm crying out and arching my back as I start spurting into the water, my heart racing and my whole body tingling. "Good boy," he says into my ear. "Such a good, gorgeous boy."

After a little while, I'm able to catch my breath again and blink my eyes back open. "Oh, Daddy," I say with a small giggle. I feel wrecked. "That was amazing."

I try and turn around so I can get my hands on his cock to return the favor, but he grips my shoulders and stops me. "What did I say?" he asks.

I frown and think back to before the orgasm. Oh! "That you were going to take care of everything."

"Exactly," he says proudly. "Good boy, baby bear. Just relax."

He runs his hands over my boneless body, kissing my neck again as I sag against him. Then he gets a hand between us and plays a little with my hole, stroking and probing it. *Ohhh.* We're not done yet, are we?

I wriggle and encourage him to finger me, letting out tiny squeaks and moans, and he pushes his way inside me. His other hand is massaging my pec, molding the flesh, and rubbing the hard, sensitive bud of my nipple. I feel like clay on a pottery wheel.

Just when my cock is starting to perk up again, he eases off and kisses my cheek.

"Daddy?" I whimper.

He laughs, but not unkindly. "The water is starting to cool, baby bear. Let's get out now and go snuggle on the bed."

"Oh, okay, then," I say, suitably mollified. In fact, I grin as he helps me to step out of the free-standing tub, my body buzzing and my sensitive parts throbbing as he towel-dries me off. The oil has left my skin feeling incredibly soft and smelling sweet.

The heating is on so high I don't feel cold at all as he leads me along the flower path again toward the bed, even though we're both still naked. The duvet is also covered in rose petals that stick to my slightly damp skin as Beckett encourages me to lie on my front with my head on the pillow.

I realize on the nightstand is a collection of flavored lubes, just like he told me, and I snort. But he picks up a tube of edible chocolate body paint and wiggles it at me. "Do you want to play, baby boy?"

My mouth goes dry. "You can play with my body however you want," I manage to utter, and I mean it. He makes me feel so fucking amazing that I'm not shy or self-conscious at all.

I want him to make me scream.

He bites his lip and moans before kissing my mouth. "Good boy. You just lie there and relax."

The chocolate is cold as he uses his finger to spread some over my hole. I have a feeling I know what's coming, but I

HJ WELCH

still yelp when his tongue licks up my crevice, then I groan in pleasure. George never liked the idea of rimming, and no other guy has done it to me either, so I've always wondered if it would be something I'd like.

I was wrong. I fucking love it.

I squirm against the bedcovers, grinding my cock on top of the mattress and gripping the duvet with both hands. *Holy fuck!* Beckett's tongue is like nothing else as he licks the chocolate from my entrance and starts to slip it past the tight ring of muscle, stretching me further in preparation for his cock.

Damn. I could come just like this. But the friction isn't quite enough against my dick, and Beckett knows it. He's also holding my hips in place, stopping me from thrusting too much as he takes his time pleasuring my hole.

Just when I think I'm going to lose my mind, he draws back, and I peek over my shoulder to see him wiping his face with his hand. Then he places his hands on either side of my ribs and tugs gently to the left.

"On your back for me now, sweetheart," he urges, helping me to flip over. I'm covered in petals, but I love it, and neither of us attempts to brush them off. Instead, Beckett gets the chocolate body paint again and strokes his length with his other hand. "Can Daddy feed you, baby bear?"

I nod frantically, probably looking like a needy slut, but I really don't care. Apparently, Beckett is eager to cram in several different sexual firsts for us this evening, and I am a thousand percent here for it.

I watch hungrily as he coats his cock with brown gooey goodness, then holds out the tips of his sticky fingers for me to suck clean. He crawls up the bed, looming over me as he angles his length into my mouth, making us both moan. I run my hands up his hairy thighs and squeeze his ass. He grips my hair and encourages me to swallow him down. The chocolate is sweet, but his cock is musky and salty with precum. I love it.

Part of me wants to get him off like this, down my throat so I choke on it. But I don't complain when he withdraws his now clean length and kisses my mouth, because I know what's going to come next.

"Good boy, so perfect," he murmurs against my lips. I love that we can both taste each other's intimate parts as we kiss.

Out of the corner of my eye, I see him reaching for one of the bottles of lube and a condom, but I don't worry about it. He told me to relax and let him take care of it, so that's what I'm going to do. I do hum as the scent of strawberries fills the air. Perfect to go with the chocolate we've already been playing with.

Between the fingering in the bath and his tongue, I'm already pretty stretched, so I'm not surprised that once he's got the condom on, he goes straight in for penetration. Sometimes I like it when I'm still quite tight. It's good to really feel the burn and be completely present in the moment, like now.

I start with my legs around his waist, but then he hooks them over his shoulders as he begins to push in deeper. I moan and cling to his tattooed biceps, loving how he's dripping sweat onto me. The room stinks like men but also with the comforting scent of candy. I love the squelching and slapping as he thrusts inside me. My body is on fire, and I cry out as he hits my prostate.

"Yes, yes, *yes*," I hiss, digging my fingers into his flesh as he claims me. Unlike last night, when we were cozy in our blanket fort, there's no dragging out this time. He's chasing his climax just as much as I'm rushing toward my second one. He leans down and kisses me hard, clashing our teeth together and biting my lip.

"Come for me, baby bear. Come for Daddy."

He reaches down and starts jerking me off. I'm so turned on it doesn't take long before I'm blinded by my high and am spurting all over my chest. I'm not even finished before he's also gnashing his teeth and throbbing inside me as he fills the condom.

He unhooks my ankles, drops his body down, and hugs me tightly as we both pant for air, and my vision slowly comes back to me. We're covered in cum and rose petals and chocolate and sweat. It's the most perfect mess I could ever have imagined.

"Baby bear," he murmurs reverently as he kisses my cheek and rubs our temples together.

I stroke his back and inhale deeply. "Thank you, Daddy," I say. "For everything."

I don't want this weekend to end because I'm so used to the future being this big, daunting thing, and my time with Beckett—while eventful and sometimes scary—has been incredible. But this is just the beginning, and what better way to commemorate it than with mind blowing sex and the sweetest cuddles after?

He leans back to take me in. We're still connected, and I love feeling him inside me as he looks at me like that. "Thank *you*," he says sincerely. "You've taught me how to hope again. How to...love."

I blink. "Love?" I whisper.

He licks his lips before leaning down to kiss me sweetly. "Maybe?" he says.

I card my fingers through his hair. "There's no rush," I assure him.

He smiles. "I know. That's the best part."

I couldn't agree more.

CHAPTER 19

Beckett

WE STICK AROUND LONG ENOUGH THE NEXT MORNING TO make sure Laurie's car has been rescued from the side of the road and towed to the garage. It felt so incredible to be able to pay for all of that for Laurie. The look of relief on his face is going to warm my heart for the whole time between now and when I'll be able to see him again. I want to take care of my boy in every way that I can, and that includes removing financial burdens that mean nothing to me but the world to him.

"Just let me know when it's all fixed, and we can come down here together and fetch it," I assure him once we're back on the road, heading home.

It was bittersweet saying good-bye to Shellridge Lodge, but I have a very strong suspicion that we'll be back there before long. It has a special place in our hearts now, after all. Besides, the cheeky bear cub, Billy, slipped me a brochure on their wedding options, which did make me laugh.

"That's so kind of you, Daddy. Thank you," Laurie says from my passenger seat. The last time he was sitting there, he'd just had his accident. It chills my blood, but it also

135

strengthens my resolve to give this new relationship everything I can.

I offer out my hand, and he immediately takes it, his skin warm against mine. I glance at the hand still on the wheel, my wedding ring glinting in the sunlight that's also bouncing off all the snow that still surrounds us.

For the first time ever, I wonder if I should take it off. Like Laurie said, there's no rush. Actually, he seems to like playing with it and is always happy to talk about Shawn. I would never, ever want to forget about my teddy bear. But there might also be a time when it's best to move on, not just for me but for whoever I'm with as well.

I hope that's Laurie. I hope we really are in this for the long run.

"It should only be a week or so until your car is ready," I comment. "But maybe after that...you might like to come and spend the weekend with me in Chicago?"

I glance over to see how his face has lit up. "I'd love that," he says breathlessly. But then his expression falls. "I wish I could offer you to come stay with me, but there's barely room for me and Mom in the house as it is, and well, I live with my mom."

I chuckle and squeeze his hand. "Don't spend even a second worrying about that, baby bear," I assure him. "Although perhaps one day I could meet your mum? No rush, of course."

"No rush," he repeats softly, his face beaming. He rubs the back of my hand with his thumb. I get the sense he's thinking, so I don't say anything until he does. "My theater group, though. Um...we're putting on this play in a couple of months that I'm doing the tech for. It's a fun murder mystery play. Maybe you could come watch that? There's a pretty good hotel in town if you'd want to get a room. I know that means spending more money, though, so—"

"Hey, hey," I say, sensing he's getting worked up. "I'd absolutely love that, sweetheart. It would be wonderful to see your play. I can figure out any details closer to the time, but a hotel sounds like a great idea. And I don't ever want you worrying about how much money I'm spending on you, okay? If I'm going to have any Daddy rules, that's a big one. Money isn't a problem for me. I earned more when I was a lawyer than I knew what to do with, so I saved a lot of it, and Shawn's inheritance from his parents also came to me not to mention his life insurance. I don't want to buy meaningless things. I want to spend it on something that matters. And that's you."

I glance away from the road to see him blushing. My sweet boy.

"Okay, Daddy," he says softly, but there's a pride in his voice that warms my heart. *Yes, Laurie, you are worth not just my time but my money. You are special.*

"I know we said a lot of things yesterday," I say, still rubbing my thumb against his knuckles. "And I kind of sprang the B-word out of the blue when we were confronting Mick. But I meant it. I'm all in, Laurie. I'd like to be your boyfriend, your Daddy, your partner, whatever word you feel comfortable with. The point is that I'm not interested in seeing anyone else. I want to be exclusive and give this relationship everything I have."

He squeezes my hand before lifting it to kiss it. "I feel the same, Daddy," he says. I hoped that was the case, but making it official gives me such joy. "You're my first proper Daddy. I can use 'partner' or 'boyfriend' around other people if they might not understand, but as far as I'm concerned, you're my Daddy, and I'm your boy."

"My baby bear," I say with a grin.

"Exactly," he agrees happily.

I hum and decide to come clean. "I think a part of me

knew I wanted to keep you from the moment I first saw you," I confess. When I glance over, I love how wide his eyes are.

"Really?" he whispers.

I chuckle ruefully. "I told myself that it was a good thing you were here meeting someone else, because I was trying to take baby steps. But secretly, I was kind of delighted that he turned out to be an arsehole."

He laughs loudly. "Don't remind me," he says good-naturedly. I'm so glad that yesterday's incident doesn't seem to have affected him too badly. What that brute did—what he said—what he threatened to *do*—still chills me to the bone. But Laurie appears to have brushed it off and is living for the moment. I need to do the same.

"As soon as I gave you the hat, gloves, and scarf, I never wanted them back," I confess as well.

He bites his lip and beams at me. "Really? I can keep them?"

I nod, loving how much he treasures such a simple gift. "I mentioned getting them back because I wanted an excuse to see you again. But now I don't need an excuse to see you or buy you presents whenever I want. Because you're my baby bear, and I'm your Daddy, so that's my job."

He hums happily and looks out the window for a while. "I think it was fate that brought us together," he announces confidently. "We should never have met, and yet when we did, the universe kept pulling us back together."

I think of Shawn in that karaoke bar when I saw him for the first time singing a tragic attempt at Shania Twain. My heart swells. We should never have been at that bar. I should never have come to this retreat. But Laurie fell into my arms because sometimes the universe really does know best.

"I believe in fate," I assure him. This time it's my turn to lift our hands and kiss the back of his. "I believe in destiny.

And I really believe that the human heart has an endless capacity for love."

He squeezes my hand, and we share a pointed look. "Amen to that," he says. "Love conquers all."

That I *truly* believe.

Epilogue

SIX MONTHS LATER – LAURIE

I DON'T HAVE THAT MUCH STUFF WITH ME, REALLY. JUST A couple of suitcases and a few boxes. It all fitted easily into my car, which is now parked in the underground lot of Beckett's building.

I can't believe I'm actually moving in with him.

Except...I can. I can't imagine it any other way, actually.

We've casually batted the idea around for a few months before we decided to just go for it. I get the feeling Beckett would have been happy to do it even sooner, but our motto is still 'no rush,' as we don't want to put pressure on each other.

But half the time that feels like a battle against our most honest desires. We've been all in on this relationship since we very first met.

Beckett did have a harder time convincing me I could really quit my terrible job, though. He's so confident I can break into the theater business here in Chicago, and is adamant about supporting me while I do so. That was a little difficult for me to accept initially without feeling guilty, but I've promised him I'm going to work my ass off and that I'll have a job in no time.

All these thoughts are swirling in my head as I pull into my new allocated spot in the garage and kill the ignition. I sit there and take a breath for a moment, sending my thanks out into the universe. I swear I'm the luckiest boy alive.

A tap on the window makes me jump out of my skin, but then I see it's Beckett looking sheepish, and I grin, even though I'm still clutching my chest. "Sorry," he blurts the moment I open the car door. He backs up so I have room to get out. "I've been down here for the last fifteen minutes, and I'm just so excited."

I laugh as I hug him tightly. The worst times over the past few months have been saying good-bye and going back to my mom's house. That's all over now. This is my home, too.

"I'm excited as well," I assure him. "The drive felt like it took forever!"

He sighs happily. "Can I help you start bringing your things up? We don't have to grab it all right away, but let's get the most important bits at least."

"Good plan," I agree. I pop the trunk and get out the first suitcase, passing it over to him.

Then I stop.

"Your wedding ring?" I blurt out, not sure how to feel. It's gone.

He holds out his left hand, extending his fingers and nodding thoughtfully as we both look at the dent in his skin. "I wondered if you'd notice at all. Of course you did. It felt like the right time, but…well…let's get upstairs, and I'd like to show you something."

I nod. If he's okay then I'm okay. But I don't want him to feel like he had to do that for me. His connection to Shawn never makes me feel threatened or that he loves me any less.

We're quiet as we ride the elevator up with my suitcases and a couple of the boxes. There's still some stuff in my back seat, but like Beckett said, that can wait. I'm familiar with the walk along the corridor to his apartment now, and even have my own key that he gave me over the summer. He wanted me to move in by October so we could celebrate all the holidays together—Halloween, Thanksgiving, Christmas, and New Year's—all the fun stuff. I've been so excited about all the traditions we're going to make together, but as we head through his front door, I can't help but feel a little anxious.

"There we go," Beckett says as he sets down my case in the living room and takes the other stuff from me. Then he slips his hand against mine. "Okay, can I show you?"

I nod. "Of course," I tell him.

He leads me into his bedroom, where I immediately notice that he's set his dresser up differently. There are two matching silver frames standing next to each other. The first has a gorgeous photo of him and Shawn on a sunny beach, hugging and holding cocktails. The second has an equally beautiful photo of me and him from this summer when we had a picnic in the park. That was the day he asked me to move in, and we're toasting with Champagne flutes.

The photos are angled around a new ornament. It's a white ceramic leafless tree attached to a small plate, which I assume is designed to hold jewelry. But on the branches there are just three matching silver rings. Actually, knowing what I do about wedding rings, they're probably platinum. I recognize one of them as Beckett's wedding band, but immediately I want to make guesses about the other two.

Instead, I hold my breath and wait for him to explain.

He comes behind me and wraps his arm around me, holding my tummy and resting his chin on my shoulder. "This is mine," he says, touching the more scuffed-looking ring before touching another one. "This was Shawn's. For a while, I wore it on a necklace. It's been in a drawer for some time. But now, I want it here so we can see it. And this one…" He touches the third and final ring that looks brand new.

"Well, this one represents you. We're all on the tree because life never stops blossoming into beautiful new things. One day, maybe you and I can wear these rings. But for now, I liked the idea of the three of them growing into something incredible in this tiny little garden."

Tears well in my eyes, and I don't fight to stop them from falling. "Oh, Beckett," I say softly. "Daddy. I'm honored. That's such a lovely idea. It's a tree of life and love."

"Absolutely," he agrees, hugging me with both arms and kissing my temple. "If that's okay with you?"

I reach out and touch Shawn's face in the photo. I wish I could have known him, but in that moment, I give him a prayer, thanking him for sharing his love with me and this amazing man. *I'll take care of him,* I promise silently. *Like he took care of you. Like he takes care of me now. He'll never be lonely again.*

Then I move my hand to touch the matching ring saved for me. I love the idea of wearing it someday.

"It's perfect with me, Daddy," I tell him sincerely.

I know that tomorrow, Beckett's planned dinner and a show for us to celebrate me officially moving in and starting my life in the city. But tonight, I'm glad it's just going to be the two of us, hidden away from the world, just like how we started our relationship.

He's my Daddy, and I don't need anything else. We have all the love we need and then some to spare.

This is the start of forever, whatever that might hold and however long it might last. I'm his, and he is mine. And with Shawn looking over us, I know it's going to be perfect.

Because love conquers all.

———

Thank you so much for reading Laurie and Beckett's story! If you enjoyed it, I hope you'll consider leaving a review.

Have you read all the other bear-licious Bears-4-U books? Make sure you grab the rest of the series here!

Keep reading to discover more Daddy books from HJ Welch and her British pen name, Helen Juliet.

DADDY'S FAIRY TALES BOX SET BY HELEN JULIET

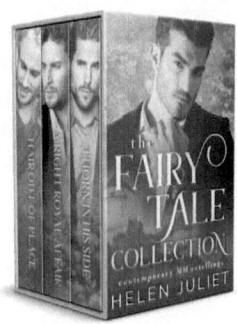

Experience Goldilocks and the Three Bears, Little Red Riding Hood, The Three Little Pigs, and Puss in Boots as you've never seen them before in this box set of contemporary adaptations! Available together for the first time, each stand alone book features a caring Daddy finding his HEA with a loving boy (or boys!)

Click here to get the Daddy's Fairy Tales eBook bundle

———

Golden

When Goldie's ex-boyfriend leaves him in serious debt with the adult entertainment company he works for, Goldie gets the chance to work off the money…in front of the camera. The idea excites him, but then his favourite throuple—Daddy, Papa, and Baby —*demand* he comes to play with them. No matter how scared he is, he can't miss this opportunity, not even when his past comes back to haunt him.

————

Wild Ride

When Red is chased into the woods, he seeks sanctuary at his estranged grandma's house. He doesn't expect to be rescued by his older brother's best friend, the man he was always madly in love with. Could Hunter be the Daddy of Red's wildest dreams? Especially when he unlocks a secret passion of Red's for beautiful lingerie. There's still a threat lurking in the woods, though, and Hunter realises he'll do anything to protect his beautiful boy.

————

Three

When three shy best friends sign up to a dating app to finally get some by the end of the year, they don't expect to all fall for the same gorgeous, slightly scary-looking Daddy. The only solution? Let him choose who he wants to bed. Except he doesn't. Daddy Wolf wants to spoil each little piggy, one after another. But when danger comes calling, will their love for each other be enough to save them all?

Includes Halloween bonus scene!

————

Nine Lives

When Charlie suddenly finds himself homeless and penniless, he decides to sell the only thing left he owns. Himself. For the very first time. Lucky for him he stumbles across Miller, the own of a London kink club, who saves him from those who would take advantage of him. As Miller discovers his inner Daddy, he also unlocks Charlie's kitten alter-ego. But with both their families meddling, will new love be enough to keep them together?

Click here to get the Daddy's Fairy Tales eBook bundle

PADDLE CREEK #1: HEAVEN SENT BY HJ WELCH

Welcome to the underdog town of Paddle Creek, where it's always the quiet ones who get up to the best kind of trouble! Join the boys, littles, kittens, dolls – you name it! – of Paddle Creek College as they meet their Daddies and find true love…with a little help from the colorful locals, of course.

Two rival jocks. One adorable nerd. A bet that changes everything.

SETH

Being captain of the Paddle Creek Panthers is my life. I wouldn't care that my grades have slipped, except it could not only cost me my shot at the pros, but now the rich kid in town has wagered that if

I don't graduate, I'll owe him *big* time. Can this gorgeous little freshman geek Gabe really save my degree and my reputation? All I know is that as soon as I laid eyes on him, I needed him. And I *don't* want to share.

MARTY

I've spent almost four years trying to get my captain Seth to notice me. He's hot as hell and knows how to boss a guy around, even one as big as me. To him, though, I'm just the team clown. But when he drags me into this graduation bet, it's no laughing matter. So why shouldn't this little cherub Gabe tutor me as well? In fact, I don't see why we can't share him in all *kinds* of ways. Seth is clearly a natural Daddy, Gabe thrives being doted on, and I'm happy to Daddy *and* be Daddied. Win-win, right?

GABE

Somehow, I've found myself standing up to the guy whose family pretty much owns Paddle Creek and put my neck on the line for two of the college's star players. Now we're spending every day together as I try and save their grades, and I don't know if I'm crazy but it's like they both *want* me. I've never had a boyfriend. I'm not even out to my overbearing parents. How could I choose between them…or do I actually have to when they *both* want to be my Daddies? After my life comes crashing down, it's their turn to come to my rescue. Maybe what me and these god-like men have isn't just a fling after all?

*Heaven Sent is a steamy, standalone MMM romance. It's the first book in the **Paddle Creek College** series, where it's always the quiet ones who get up to the best kind of trouble. This book features a geek tutoring two hot jocks, two hot jocks tutoring a geek in a completely different way, a trash panda with a heart of gold, a human ice cream sundae, a revenge curse, and a guaranteed HEA with absolutely no cliffhanger.*

Click here to get the Heaven Sent eBook

Also Available

PADDLE CREEK #2: YES, SIR BY HJ WELCH

Two men. Two secrets. Can true love set them free?

BENEDICT

Just one more year, then I can go back to my beloved Oxford University and leave this tiny town behind me. Teaching is my passion, but I have other desires that I know would get me fired if anyone found out. The only trouble is, my new TA is pushing all my buttons and I'm not sure he even realizes what calling me Sir does to me. That's nothing, however, compared to when he starts calling me Daddy.

JACKSON

Have I got hots for teacher? Oh, yes. Messing around is off the table, though, so in a way it's safe to flirt with him and see him lose that stiff upper lip. It's not like he'd be interested in me anyway if he ever discovered what I love wearing under my clothes. Tough guys like me shouldn't like satin and lace. They shouldn't want to feel pretty. But Sir makes me feel gorgeous, and I want to be *such* a good boy for him.

*Yes, Sir is a steamy, standalone MM romance. It's the second book in the **Paddle Creek College** series, where it's always the quiet ones who get up to the best kind of trouble. This book features two people learning they don't have to be ashamed of who they are, a sassy brat who really wants to behave, a master in the bedroom who's a caring Daddy at heart, role playing so good it could win an Oscar, and a guaranteed HEA with absolutely no cliffhanger.*

Click here to get the Yes, Sir eBook

PADDLE CREEK #3: LITTLE PLEASURES BY HJ WELCH

One jaded Daddy. One brand new boy. A fake relationship that becomes all too real.

RUBEN

When my life-long best friend asks me to keep an eye on his stepbrother, of course I agree. Except he's a young man now, not a kid, and he's tugging at every single one of my Daddy heartstrings. Xander has just moved back into town and between his masters degree, part-time work, and hellish stepmother, he's stressing himself into knots. It's a long time since a boy interested me, but I just want to protect Xander from the whole world.

XANDER

It's bad enough I have to move back to Paddle Creek with my awful stepmom, but now my stepbrother's best friend has decided he has to look after me—even pretending to be my new boyfriend to keep my stepmother off my back. What Ruben doesn't know is that I've been in love with him for as long as I can remember and spending so much time with him is torture. Until it isn't. I can't believe that he's interested in me and even wants to be my Daddy, unlocking something in me I never knew was there. But when my stepmom goes too far, can I rely on Ruben to be there for me when no one else in my life ever has?

Little Pleasures is a steamy, standalone MM romance. It's the third book in the Paddle Creek College series, where it's always the quiet ones who get up to the best kind of trouble. This book features a Daddy introducing a boy to his inner little, the most loyal doggy best friend, a lot of dinosaurs, a heart-stopping rescue, and a guaranteed HEA with absolutely no cliffhanger.

Click here to pre-order the Little Pleasures eBook

About the Author

HJ Welch is an author of contemporary MM romance series, including the international bestselling Pine Cove series. She lives just outside of London with her husband and two balls of fluff that occasionally pretend to be cats. She began writing at an early age, later honing her craft online in the world of fanfiction on sites like Wattpad. Fifteen years and over half a million words later, she sought out original MM novels to read. By the end of 2016 she had written her first book of her own, and in 2017 she achieved her lifelong dream of becoming a full-time author. When she's not writing she's usually dancing, singing, filming music videos, taking long walks, working on jigsaw puzzles, drinking prosecco, or talking about Eurovision.

She also writes contemporary British MM fairy tale adaptations as Helen Juliet.

You can contact Helen via the following:
 Newsletter: https://www.subscribepage.com/helenjuliet
 Website – www.hjwelch.com
 Facebook Group – Helen's Jewels
 Instagram – @helenjwrites
 Twitter – @helenjwrites
 Book Bub – @HJWelchAuthor
 Facebook Page – @HJWelchAuthor

www.ingramcontent.com/pod-product-compliance
Lightning Source LLC
Chambersburg PA
CBHW051230210726
48290CB00003B/887